THE DEMON
HEADMASTER

TOTAL
CONTROL

The most hypnotic villain of all . . .

Get ready for adventure and intrigue.

Prepare to fall under his spell.

Do not try to resist . . .

**Are you ready to meet the Demon Headmaster? Here's a taste of what's to come . . .**

'Lizzie Warren, you are a troublemaker,' said the voice.

'I'm not!' Lizzie said. 'I've never—'

'SILENCE!' The sound boomed through the empty air, almost deafening them. 'You are a troublemaker. Last term, you were almost excluded for fighting another student.'

'I had to do it!' Lizzie said fiercely. 'Blake kept bullying Tyler. I couldn't let him—'

The voice interrupted again and this time it was hard and cold. Like ice. 'Do not waste time making excuses. Stop talking and listen to me.'

Tyler started shaking and Lizzie put her arm round him. 'It's OK,' she whispered.

Tyler didn't answer. He just turned very pale and pointed across the room.

The air next to the desk had suddenly started shimmering.

It was only a small patch at first, a tiny disturbance, so small it was hardly visible. But it began to spread, growing slowly larger and brighter. Thickening and changing colour. Gradually a shape formed in front of them, appearing out of thin air.

They found themselves looking at a tall man in dark glasses. He was dressed in black, from head to foot, but his hair and his skin were very pale, as though all the colour had been drained out of them.

Tyler gave a little, trembling gasp. 'What is it?' he whispered. 'Is he really here?'

'I think . . . it's a hologram,' Lizzie whispered back. She could hear her voice trembling too.

'You are not required to speak,' the man said sharply. 'You are useless troublemakers, with nothing valuable to say.' His eyes were still hidden, but his mouth curved into a small, tight smile. 'But you will not be useless for long. This school will turn you into useful members of society.' He lifted a hand to take off his glasses. 'Look at me. Both of you.'

Lizzie shivered. She didn't want to look, but before she could turn away the dark glasses came off—and she found herself staring into two green eyes like deep pools of water. Deep, deep . . .

*No*, she thought dizzily. *I won't look . . . He can't make me . . .*

But she didn't finish the thought. Her mind clouded over and everything dissolved in the depths of those cold green eyes. She was falling, falling, falling . . .

And then her mind went blank.

# OXFORD
### UNIVERSITY PRESS

Great Clarendon Street, Oxford OX2 6DP
Oxford University Press is a department of the University of Oxford.
It furthers the University's objective of excellence in research, scholarship,
and education by publishing worldwide. Oxford is a registered trade mark
of Oxford University Press in the UK and in certain other countries

Database right Oxford University Press (maker)

First published 2017

British Library Cataloguing in Publication Data

Data available

ISBN: 978-0-19-274574-3

1 3 5 7 9 10 8 6 4 2

Printed in Great Britain

Paper used in the production of this book is a natural,
recyclable product made from wood grown in sustainable forests.
The manufacturing process conforms to the environmental
regulations of the country of origin.

# THE DEMON HEADMASTER

# TOTAL CONTROL

## GILLIAN CROSS

OXFORD
UNIVERSITY PRESS

# CONTENTS

# 1

# NIGHTMARE

The night before they went back to school, Tyler had a nightmare. Lizzie heard him whimpering—because she'd been awake for hours. She slipped out of bed and crept across to his bedroom.

'You're just dreaming,' she whispered. 'Wake up, Ty.'

She turned on the light next to his bed and he sat up suddenly, with the covers pulled close to his chin. 'Something horrible,' he said. 'Coming to get me.'

Lizzie could see him trembling. 'Was it Blake?' Tyler didn't answer and she patted his hand. 'Don't worry. It was only a dream.'

'I wish we didn't have to go back to school,' Tyler whispered. 'I want to miss the rest of this term too. I wish we'd stayed in America.'

'That was never going to happen,' Lizzie said. 'We only went for Mum's operation. But it worked, didn't it? Her heart's getting better every day and she'll soon be properly well again. Then you can tell her about Blake, if he's still being horrible. But you never know—maybe he's changed while we've been away.'

'He'll never change,' Tyler muttered. 'I bet he's got worse.'

But he lay down again and let Lizzie tuck him in.

She waited just outside the door until it sounded as if he was asleep. Then she went back to her own room.

But she didn't sleep. She lay awake for another hour, staring up at the ceiling and worrying about Tyler. He'd been fine in America, the way he used to be, before Blake started bullying him. He knew they were there to help Mum get better, so he'd never moaned about having to hang around in hospital. Just sat there, very quietly, practising his magic tricks.

If only they didn't have to go back to school . . .

## 2
# ETHAN

Next morning, while Lizzie and Tyler were still in bed, a boy called Ethan wheeled his bike out of a shed on the other side of town.

His Auntie Beryl was there too, to make sure he left on time. 'Don't be late,' she said, fluttering round him. 'You mustn't miss a minute of school. You're so *fortunate* to be there!'

Ethan put on his helmet, without answering. She said the same thing every morning. Every. Single. Morning.

'It's such a *wonderful* school!' Auntie Beryl cooed. 'You were lucky to get a place, you know. They said they were full when I phoned up. I had to work really hard to persuade them.'

*I wish you hadn't,* Ethan thought. He'd liked his old school. It was a bit boring, but he'd had a couple of good friends there—two other computer geeks he could really talk to. They'd been surprised when he'd left at half-term.

It was all Auntie Beryl's idea. She'd decided to move him as soon as she found the new school website—and saw their video on YouTube. That was peculiar, because she was super-cautious. It normally took her weeks to make up her mind about anything. But from the moment she saw that video she'd been obsessed with getting him into the school. He'd heard her on the phone, begging them to find him a place. And she'd spent the whole of half-term going on about how great it was.

Well, he'd been there for two weeks now and he just didn't get it. It wasn't a great school. It was—weird. Every kid seemed to be following a different timetable, so it was hard getting to know people. And he'd had the same homework every night.

Running.

What kind of homework was that?

He had to do a long run every day. That meant he hardly had any free time to go on the computer. And last night he'd had to watch a video too. It must have been boring, because he couldn't remember anything about it.

But Auntie Beryl still thought it was a wonderful school. She didn't listen when he told her what it was really like. As he did up his helmet, she was humming happily and, when he was ready, she patted his hand and beamed at him.

'Off you go, then. Have another brilliant day. I just wish it was me!'

*I wish it was you as well*, Ethan thought gloomily, as he cycled off.

It took him half an hour to cycle to school. He arrived fifteen minutes early, locked his bike in the cycle shed, and joined the line of kids trudging round to the students' entrance.

In the beginning, he'd tried talking to some of them. But they never said anything back, except, 'Another day at school! Isn't that great?' No one ever, *ever* moaned. And no one asked his name. Even the kids in his class hardly knew who he was.

He trailed into the classroom, still ten minutes early. He was always one of the first, because Auntie Beryl was so keen to get him to school. This morning there were only three other people there before him. A couple of boys (Harry and Josh?—or was it Simon and Jude?) and the tall, bouncy girl called Angelika, who ran the coffee stall in the canteen.

She was always early too, because her mum was the Deputy Head.

Miss Wellington came in five minutes later. She nodded solemnly as she checked Ethan's homework log.

'That's excellent. Your running times keep getting better. And I have some good news for you today. You won't be doing maths this morning. You're moving on to a personal timetable.'

Ethan frowned. Maths was one of his favourite subjects. 'So what am I doing instead?'

Miss Wellington smiled, as if she was offering him a huge treat. 'Football!' she said.

'*Football?*'

Miss Wellington nodded. 'Just you, out of the whole class. Isn't that an honour?'

'But—' Ethan was speechless. He was rubbish at football. At his old school, the team that got him had always groaned. In a nice way—but loudly. Why would anyone choose *him*, out of the whole class, for extra football? 'Must be a mistake,' he muttered.

Miss Wellington didn't see his expression, because she was busy turning on the computer. 'There's no mistake,' she said briskly. 'Special instructions from the Headmaster. You have to go down to the changing room straight after registration.'

'But—I haven't got any kit.'

'Kit will be provided.' Miss Wellington looked away and started tapping at her keyboard, logging on. **V-.-W-e-l-l-i-n-g-t-o-n-.-G-e-o-g-r-a-p-h-y** and then **I-c-e-c-r-e-a-m-1-2-3**. Ethan was so dazed he just stood watching her—until she turned round impatiently. 'Go and sit down. I need to take the register.'

He walked to his seat, feeling gloomy. The running homework was bad enough, but this was *much worse*. And when he looked through the window, he could see frost on the football pitches. He was going to *freeze*.

He was so busy staring out of the window that he missed his name on the register. Angelika nudged him with a sharp elbow.

'Stop dreaming!' she hissed.

'S-sorry,' Ethan muttered. He looked up at Miss Wellington. 'Yes.'

'Thank you,' Miss Wellington said gravely. 'I knew you were here, of course. But things must be done properly. Those are the Headmaster's instructions.' She looked down at the register again and called the last name. 'Lizzie Warren?'

'IN AMERICA!' shouted everyone except Ethan.

Miss Wellington shook her head. 'Isn't she back yet? I thought she was supposed to be here today.' She closed the register and nodded at Ethan. 'Off you go then. Have a great morning.'

Ethan picked up his bag and trailed out of the classroom.

 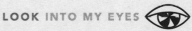

# 3

# EVERY STUDENT IS A STAR

Lizzie and Tyler were still on their way to school. They'd overslept, because of waking up in the night, and Dad hadn't realized, because he'd been so busy looking after Mum. While Ethan was sitting in registration, they were only just leaving their flat. They raced out of the block, but when they reached the road, Lizzie slowed down.

'Better go carefully,' she muttered. 'In case—*you* know.'

'You mean—*him*?' Tyler shivered. It wouldn't be the first time they found Blake waiting for them.

'Hang on while I look.' Lizzie stopped at the corner and peered round into the High Street.

There was no sign of Blake. Actually, there was no sign of *anyone*. The High Street was almost empty. Where were all the other kids who usually trailed in late? Lizzie couldn't see anyone under fifty.

'Maybe we've got it wrong,' she said hopefully. 'Maybe there *isn't* any school today!'

Tyler sighed and shook his head. 'Yes, there is. I looked out of the window while I was eating my breakfast. There were lots of people on their way to school. Come on.' He put his head down and started tramping up the High Street.

Lizzie stared at his back. *He's so small,* she thought.

She clenched her fists and ran after him, wishing she'd learnt kick-boxing while they were in America.

Tyler was just ahead of her as they went round the last corner, into Hazelbrook Road. When he saw the school, he stopped dead. 'Look,' he whispered. '*Look!*'

Lizzie stopped beside him, staring with her mouth open.

The school gates were straight ahead of them. As usual. But they weren't the old wooden gates that had always been there. They were brand-new metal ones, twice as big as the old gates. And arching over them was a huge sky-blue noticeboard that said:

# HAZELBROOK ACADEMY
## where every student is a star

The new gates were painted gleaming black, to match the words on the sign—and they were shut tightly.

'It looks as though they're locked,' Lizzie said. 'Maybe we can't get in.'

'We have to *try*,' Tyler muttered. He walked up to the gates and pushed at them. They didn't open, but a loud voice sounded from a speaker just under the sign.

'Good morning, Tyler,' it said. 'You are two months, two weeks, fifteen minutes, and twenty seconds late.'

Lizzie nearly fell over. That sounded like Mrs Harriman, the school secretary. Except that Mrs Harriman was always friendly and flustered. This voice sounded super-efficient.

Tyler tilted his head back, looking up at the speaker. 'We've—um—we've been in America,' he said.

'Dad's written us a letter.' Lizzie took it out of her pocket and waved it.

'You'd better not waste any more time,' said Mrs Harriman's voice. 'Come straight to Reception. There will be a welcomer to greet you there.'

There was a buzz and the gleaming gates swung open in front of them.

'What's a welcomer?' Tyler whispered to Lizzie. 'Why do we need one?'

Lizzie shrugged. 'There's only one way to find out. Come on.'

She pushed Tyler through the gates ahead of her. As she followed him, she glanced over her shoulder. The moment they were inside, the gates swung shut again, with a soft little *click*. Lizzie shivered as she and Tyler headed for the main entrance.

They climbed the steps and the big glass doors opened in front of them. From inside came a solemn, polite voice.

'Good morning, Lizzie. Good morning, Tyler. It's an honour to welcome you to your first day at the *new* Hazelbrook Academy. The school where every student is a star.' The welcomer gave them a wide, friendly smile.

He looked like the perfect student. His face was scrubbed clean, his hair was slicked back, and his sky-blue tie was neatly knotted at the front of his gleaming white shirt. For a second, Lizzie almost didn't recognize him.

Then she felt Tyler shiver beside her. And she saw the bulldog face behind the smile. The broad, hefty shoulders and the brutal, heavy ridge of the welcomer's eyebrows.

It was *Blake*.

She shuddered, before she could stop herself, but Blake didn't seem to notice. He stepped back and waved a hand, ushering them through the doors. When they were inside, he made another little speech.

'As you can see, our school has been wonderfully transformed. You were unlucky to miss the induction on Day One of Hazelbrook Academy (where every student is a star). But Mrs Maron will see you now, to help you catch up with the rest of us.'

'Mrs Maron?' Lizzie frowned. 'Who's that?'

'Our new Deputy Head,' said Blake. 'Appointed by the Headmaster himself. Let me take you to her office.' He set off along the corridor, glancing back over his shoulder to make sure Lizzie and Tyler were following.

'Head*master*?' whispered Tyler.

That was different as well. What had happened to Miss Sefton, the old Head?

Blake led them past the hall and knocked on a door with a shiny new nameplate.

Mrs B. Maron—Deputy Head

They heard the sound of sharp high heels clicking across the room. The door flew open and a brisk, bright voice said, 'Lizzie, Tyler—good morning! I'm delighted to welcome you to the all-new Hazelbrook Academy.'

Mrs Maron was tall and elegant. Her smile was gleaming. Her neat blonde hair shone and her black shoes had heels like daggers. *Beata Maron: Deputy Head, Public Relations* said the badge on her smart sky-blue jacket.

She waved Lizzie and Tyler into her office. 'Wait there, Blake,' she said. 'I'll need you in a moment, to escort Lizzie and Tyler to the Headmaster's office.' She shut the door, marched across the room and looked down at her computer. 'Before you see the Headmaster, I need to update your records. We don't seem to have your parents' email addresses.'

'They haven't got a computer,' Lizzie said. 'Or a smartphone.'

'Not any more,' said Tyler. 'We had to spend all our money going to America, for Mum's—'

Mrs Maron held up her hand to stop him talking. 'That is not acceptable. It's essential for parents to have access to the school website at all times. I'll have to sort something out.'

She gave a brisk nod and tapped at her computer keyboard. Then she marched back to the door and opened it. Blake was still outside, exactly where they'd left him, standing to attention.

'Take Lizzie and Tyler to the Headmaster's office,' Mrs Maron said. 'Then return to your classroom and continue with your personal timetable.' She waved Lizzie and Tyler out of her room and shut the door smartly behind them.

'Please follow me,' Blake said. 'The Headmaster's office is this way.'

He started down the corridor and Lizzie and Tyler turned to follow him. But they had only taken a couple of steps when there was a strange whirring noise behind them. Looking over her shoulder, Lizzie saw a small sky-blue shape hovering in the air. It was high up, near the ceiling, and it had spindly black legs and a round, bright spot at the front—like a single, gleaming eye. For one horrible moment, she thought it was a giant insect.

Then it moved towards them, and she realized what she was looking at. 'It's a *machine!*' she said.

Blake glanced back and nodded. 'The Headmaster's eyes are everywhere,' he said.

'The Headmaster's *eyes*?' Tyler stared at him. 'What do you mean?'

Blake pointed up at the little blue machine. 'Those are a key part of school security.' He recited the words as if he was reading them. 'They monitor behaviour and ensure that pupils are obedient and safe at all times.'

Lizzie shivered. 'You mean—they're spy drones?'

Just for a second, Blake's eyes flickered, as if she'd surprised him. Then he gave another of his polite smiles. 'Safety and security are essential to efficient learning,' he said, as he started down the corridor again.

Lizzie caught hold of Tyler's hand and gave it a squeeze. 'Maybe they'll keep you safe from *him*,' she whispered.

Blake stopped just ahead of them, outside a door that said *Headmaster*. Just at that moment, another

LOOK INTO MY EYES

boy came hurrying round the corner beyond him. He bumped into Blake, catching him off balance, and sent him staggering backwards. Blake crashed into the wall on the other side of the corridor, with a loud thud.

*Oh no!* Lizzie thought. *Now there's going to be trouble.* No one got away with pushing Blake around. Certainly not this boy. He was small and wiry—not much bigger than Tyler. He wouldn't stand a chance when Blake started on him.

But that didn't happen.

Blake blinked and stood up, straightening his tie. Then he looked apologetically at the strange boy. 'My fault for being in your way,' he said. 'Did I hurt you? Sorry, I don't know your name.'

'Ethan,' the boy mumbled. 'I'm Ethan—and I'm fine. It was my fault for not looking.'

'Don't worry about it,' Blake said politely. 'Do you need any help?'

The boy looked up and down the corridor. (Was he new? Lizzie was sure she'd never seen him before.) 'I'm supposed to be going to the changing rooms,' he muttered. 'But I don't know where they are.'

'Go down to the end of this corridor.' Blake pointed the way. 'Then turn left and straight on through the double doors. I'm sorry I can't take you there, but—'

'It's OK,' the boy said quickly. 'I know the way now.' He set off down the corridor.

'Go carefully,' Blake called after him.

Lizzie and Tyler looked at each other. What was going on? How come Blake was being kind and helpful?

It was creepy. Lizzie kept waiting for him to change back to his old self and start thumping someone, but he just went on smiling. Was he—?

She never finished that thought. Because the door to the Headmaster's office swung open suddenly and a deep voice spoke from inside.

'Lizzie Warren and Tyler Warren, come in now.'

'Go on!' Blake gave them each a gentle push.

They stumbled through the doorway—into an empty room. There was a desk on the far side, with a single chair behind it, but no one was sitting at the desk. No one was anywhere to be seen. It was just a square, empty room, like a box.

Tyler edged closer to Lizzie, and she caught hold of his hand and squeezed it tightly. 'Don't worry,' she whispered. 'It'll be all right.'

'Silence!' said the deep voice they had heard before. 'I shall tell you if you are required to speak.'

The sound seemed to be coming from all around them. There had to be speakers somewhere, but Lizzie couldn't see them. It felt as if the room was talking.

'Lizzie Warren, you are a troublemaker,' said the voice.

'I'm not!' Lizzie said. 'I've never—'

'SILENCE!' The sound boomed through the empty air, almost deafening them. 'You are a troublemaker. Last term, you were almost excluded for fighting another student.'

'I had to do it!' Lizzie said fiercely. 'Blake kept bullying Tyler. I couldn't let him—'

The voice interrupted again and this time it was hard and cold. Like ice. 'Do not waste time making excuses. Stop talking and listen to me.'

Tyler started shaking and Lizzie put her arm round him. 'It's OK,' she whispered.

Tyler didn't answer. He just turned very pale and pointed across the room.

The air next to the desk had suddenly started shimmering.

It was only a small patch at first, a tiny disturbance, so small it was hardly visible. But it began to spread, growing slowly larger and brighter. Thickening and changing colour. Gradually a shape formed in front of them, appearing out of thin air.

They found themselves looking at a tall man in dark glasses. He was dressed in black, from head to foot, but his hair and his skin were very pale, as though all the colour had been drained out of them.

Tyler gave a little, trembling gasp. 'What is it?' he whispered. 'Is he really here?'

'I think . . . it's a hologram,' Lizzie whispered back. She could hear her voice trembling too.

'You are not required to speak,' the man said sharply. 'You are useless troublemakers, with nothing valuable to say.' His eyes were still hidden, but his mouth curved into a small, tight smile. 'But you will not be useless for long. This school will turn you into useful members of society.' He lifted a hand to take off his glasses. 'Look at me. Both of you.'

Lizzie shivered. She didn't want to look, but before

she could turn away the dark glasses came off—and she found herself staring into two green eyes like deep pools of water. Deep, deep . . .

*No,* she thought dizzily. *I won't look . . . He can't make me . . .*

But she didn't finish the thought. Her mind clouded over and everything dissolved in the depths of those cold green eyes. She was falling, falling, falling . . .

And then her mind went blank.

# 4

# FOOTBALL

Ethan had almost reached the changing rooms. But he wasn't thinking about football. He was thinking about the two kids he'd seen outside the Headmaster's office.

*Who were they?* He'd never seen them before, but they had to be brother and sister. They both had the same curly brown hair and baggy old sweatshirts. All the other kids in the school were super-smart, but those two looked poor and scruffy.

And *scared*.

That was why he couldn't stop thinking about them. When he bumped into the other boy—the huge one—those two had gasped, as if he was going to get thumped. But Huge Boy couldn't have been nicer. So why were they nervous?

Was it because they were waiting to see the Headmaster?

Ethan suddenly remembered how *he'd* felt two weeks ago, waiting outside that office on his first day at Hazelbrook. He'd been nervous too. He'd actually shivered when he'd heard the Headmaster's voice, calling him inside. But then—

He frowned. That was weird. He remembered the waiting all right. But he couldn't remember anything about what had happened inside the office. What *had* happened then? He needed to think . . .

But he didn't think. He'd reached the boys' changing room. And when he opened the door, he forgot about everything else. Because there had to be some mistake. All the boys were much older than he was. And about twice as big.

'I—er—sorry,' he muttered.

He started backing out again, but the PE teacher ran forward and grabbed his arm. 'You're Ethan Prendergast, aren't you?' he said.

Ethan nodded. 'Yes, but I'm not—'

The teacher shook his head impatiently. 'Don't waste time, boy. We've been waiting for you. I'm Mr Wasu—and your kit's in that locker over there. Get it on as fast as you can.'

The other boys were staring at Ethan and a couple of them sniggered. They obviously thought there was a mistake too. Mr Wasu turned and glared round the changing room.

'None of that!' he snapped. 'Ethan's our new striker and you'll give him your full support—or you're off the team. Now get out on the field, all of you.'

Ethan stared at Mr Wasu as the others ran outside. 'But I don't—' he stammered. 'I can't—it's a mistake.'

'There's no mistake,' Mr Wasu said impatiently. 'I've had special instructions about you. Direct from the Headmaster. So get your kit on. I'll give you two minutes to be out on the field.'

He followed the other boys out of the changing room and Ethan went across and opened his locker.

Inside was a pair of brand-new boots and a set of sky-blue football kit. He stared miserably at them, hoping they wouldn't fit. If the shorts fell down when he put them on—or the boots were too big to walk in—then he wouldn't be *able* to play.

But everything fitted perfectly. Even the boots were right. (That was creepy. How did they know his size?) He laced them up, took a deep breath, and opened the door that led outside. *Here goes,* he thought miserably, as he jogged out on to the football field. He felt totally wretched.

But that only lasted for a few seconds. The moment he stepped on to the pitch, everything changed.

His mind went completely blank.

The next thing he knew, he was walking off the football field. And the two reserves were jumping up and down on the touchline.

'That was a brilliant goal!' said one of them. 'Never seen anything like it!'

'Piotr needs to watch himself,' said the other with a cheeky grin. 'Or you'll be captain instead of him!'

When the other footballers heard that, they started laughing, and Piotr clapped Ethan on the back.

'Looks as though we're lucky to have you,' he said.

'But I—' *I don't remember anything*, Ethan was going to say. *I don't know what you're talking about.*

But somehow the words didn't come out. Suddenly, his mind drifted off and he blinked at Piotr. What was it he'd meant to say? He had no idea.

Mr Wasu came hurrying into the changing room. 'Well done, all of you. Especially you, Ethan. Now get on and have your shower. You've just got time before lunch.'

'*Lunch*?' Ethan stared at him.

'We've been out on the field all morning. Didn't you realize?' Mr Wasu laughed. 'You *must* have been enjoying yourself! Bet you're looking forward to tomorrow's game.'

'I'm playing again tomorrow?' Ethan said.

This time it was Mr Wasu who stared. 'You know you are. I've just told you—out there on the field.'

'I don't—' *I don't remember*. Ethan started to say it, but the same thing happened again. As if his brain had changed into a mist and just . . . floated away. What was happening?

He wanted to sit very still and think about it, but Mr Wasu was hassling him to have a shower. 'Come on, boy. You don't want to miss lunch.'

'Yeah, come on, Ethan,' said Piotr. 'I'll race you.'

Ethan hauled himself off the bench and followed the others into the showers.

When they came out, the lunch bell was ringing. The other boys were all in the second sitting, because they were older, but Ethan had to go straight to the canteen. He was already late. By the time he got there, the queue stretched out of the door.

He joined the end of it and read the menu as they shuffled towards the counter.

TOMATO SOUP
FISH PIE
TOAD-IN-THE-HOLE
VEGETABLE CHILLI AND SALAD

None of those sounded great. But he was really hungry today. Maybe he'd have the fish pie—and then treat himself to a big hot chocolate from Angelika's coffee stall.

As he reached for a tray, he realized he was standing right behind the two scruffy kids he'd seen outside the Headmaster's office.

'Hi,' he said. 'Can you see what the fish pie's like?'

The girl peered at the counter ahead of them. 'It seems pretty good. Considering.' Then she turned and looked back at him. 'Hello,' she said. 'We saw you before, didn't we? You crashed into Blake.'

Ethan grinned at her. 'He's *massive*, isn't he? Good thing he doesn't get angry.'

The girl gave him an odd look. 'You're new, aren't you?' she said.

Ethan nodded. 'I'm in Miss Wellington's tutor group.'

'Hey—so am I.' She grinned. 'I'm Lizzie Warren.'

'You've been in America!' Ethan said.

Lizzie nodded and her brother turned round to join in. 'I was there too,' he said. 'I'm Tyler Warren. This is our first day back at school.'

'Good?' said Ethan.

Lizzie hesitated. 'It's all a bit—'

Ethan never found out what she meant to say next. The queue moved again and they finally reached the counter. Suddenly, in the middle of what she was saying, Lizzie whirled round and snatched at the big pot of tomato soup standing next to them.

She heaved it up, out of its slot, and threw it across the room, sending hot soup shooting everywhere. The empty pot clattered on to the floor and people started yelling and trying to catch hold of her, but she didn't seem to care. She spun back to the counter and grabbed at the tray of vegetable chilli.

'Lizzie!' Tyler was shouting at her. 'What are you doing? STOP!'

Behind the counter, the two dinner ladies were in shock. One of them started screaming and the other one turned white, paralysed with horror.

Lizzie didn't seem to hear them. She raced round the canteen, sending the vegetable chilli spraying out in a huge arc. Then she charged back to the counter, snatching the toad-in-the-hole and the fish pie and flinging them up in the air.

'No!' Tyler yelled.

Lizzie reached for the big jug of thick, brown gravy. The dinner ladies tried to stop her, but they couldn't reach across the counter, and the other kids were all busy laughing and filming her on their phones. There was soup on the floor, fish on the ceiling—

And gravy all over Mrs Maron, who had just walked into the canteen.

'NO!' wailed Tyler, when he saw her furious face.

Lizzie dropped the last dish on to the floor with a loud clatter. Then she blinked and looked round, with a puzzled frown.

# 5

# LIZZIE IN TROUBLE

What had happened to the canteen? Lizzie was totally baffled. The floor was a sea of tomato soup. There was vegetable chilli on the walls, the people in front of her had fish pie splattered all over them, and she could see pieces of toad-in-the hole stuck up on the ceiling.

Not to mention the big splashes of gravy on the front of Mrs Maron's smart sky-blue suit.

How had all that happened? She'd been standing quietly in the queue, talking to that new boy, Ethan, and then she'd looked round—and there was food *everywhere*.

'I don't get it,' she muttered to Tyler. 'What on earth—?'

She didn't get any further, because Mrs Maron came marching towards her, with her sharp heels stabbing into the lumps of food on the floor.

'You wicked girl!' she shouted. Her right hand was shaking, as if she wanted to slap Lizzie's face. 'You wicked, *stupid* girl! What did you think you were doing?'

'*Me?*' Lizzie said. 'But I didn't—'

'You did!' That was Mrs Foster, the cross dinner lady. She leaned over the counter, shaking her fist at Lizzie. 'What's the point of lying? We all saw you do it.'

'And the food—' wailed Mrs Khan, the nice dinner

lady. 'Look at all the *food* you've wasted.'

'Never mind the food!' Mrs Maron shrieked. 'What about the *inspection*? We've got inspectors coming on Friday, for a *very important visit*. They mustn't find out about this.' She glared round at all the people with phones in their hands. 'Put those away. *NOW!*'

She waited until she saw it was being done. Then she waved her hand at Lizzie. 'And you—clear up this mess! *AT ONCE!*'

'B-but I didn't— Lizzie stuttered. 'It w-wasn't—'

Then she saw Tyler's face. He was shaking his head at her, with his face scrunched up as if he was going to cry.

'It *was*, Lizzie,' he whispered. 'It was *you*.'

'It certainly was!' yelled another voice. A tall, blonde girl came running across the canteen, looking as if she was about to burst into tears. 'You threw vegetable chilli all over my coffee machine. I'm going to lose a whole day's business cleaning it up. It'll wreck my business plan.'

Lizzie blinked at her. Who was she? And what did she mean about a business plan?

Mrs Maron put an arm round the girl's shoulders. 'Don't worry, Angelika. This Lizzie girl will be doing all the cleaning. Starting *now*.'

Lizzie stared. It felt as if the whole world had suddenly stopped making sense. *Why was everyone expecting her to clear up the mess?* Mrs Khan came out from behind the counter, carrying a bucket, a shovel, and a stiff broom.

Tyler took the bucket and smiled at Lizzie. 'I'll help you,' he whispered. 'Come on, Liz. You've got to do it.'

Mrs Khan put the other things down and patted Lizzie's shoulder. 'You'll feel better when it's done,' she said kindly. 'Shovel up what you can and then I'll bring you a mop.'

'What about our dinner?' said Angelika. 'Are we going to miss it—just because *she* went crazy?'

'Of course not!' Mrs Maron said briskly. 'Hazelbrook Academy always provides what its students need. Mrs Khan, Mrs Foster—please serve up the rest of the food in the kitchen.'

'What about the second sitting?' grumbled Mrs Foster. 'They won't like it if there's nothing left for them.'

Mrs Maron waved a hand. 'They can have pizzas. I'll go and order some now.' She bustled off, looking for the number on her phone.

Lizzie stared at the shovel. And the bucket. And the mess. 'Better get going,' she muttered. 'Shall we start up the far end, Ty?'

'I'll help too,' said a voice.

It was that new boy. Ethan. He grinned at Lizzie and picked up the broom. 'You hold the shovel and I'll sweep stuff into it. If Tyler follows us round with the bucket, you can empty the shovel into that. OK?' Before Lizzie could even say thank you, he was over on the far side of the canteen. Lizzie and Tyler ran across to join him.

Just beside where he was sweeping, there was a shiny new coffee machine behind the counter. Tyler nodded at it. 'What's that doing there? We didn't have one of those last term.'

'It's Angelika's stall,' Ethan said. He pointed at the notice above the counter.

# ANGELIC DRINKS
## COFFEES, TEAS, HOT CHOCOLATE, AND SMOOTHIES
### TREAT YOURSELF TODAY!!!

'You mean—it's like a business?' Tyler said. 'In *school*?'

'I guess so.' Ethan shrugged. 'It's what Angelika does. Isn't that how this school works? Everyone has something they're specially good at.'

Lizzie had no idea what he meant. It was just one more thing that didn't make sense. Like Blake being a welcomer. And all that food everywhere . . .

*How could she have thrown it without remembering? Had she had some kind of fit?* She wanted to ask Ethan and Tyler, but Ethan was already working hard, sweeping the spilt chilli into a big, messy pile. And Tyler was looking anxiously at her, as if he was afraid of what she might do next. She sighed and picked up the shovel.

When the bucket was full, Tyler went off to empty it, and Ethan leaned on the broom and looked at Lizzie.

'What were you thinking,' he said carefully, 'when you were chucking all that food around?'

Lizzie bit her lip. That was the really frightening

thing. 'I don't—' she started.

*I don't remember*, she was going to say. But somehow . . . she lost track of the words, as if her mind had suddenly drifted off. For a moment, she hardly even knew where she was.

When she came back down to earth, Ethan was staring at her, looking thoughtful. 'Maybe we should talk,' he said slowly. 'Maybe—'

But before he could say anything else, the bell started ringing for the end of First Lunch. All around them, people jumped up from the tables and started moving.

'Not you, Lizzie Warren!' bellowed Mrs Foster from behind the counter. 'You're not going anywhere until all that mess is cleared up.'

Lizzie sighed and picked up the shovel. She thought Tyler would stay and help her, but as he came back with the bucket he glanced up at the clock.

'Sorry, Liz,' he muttered. 'I have to go.'

'But it's break,' Lizzie said. '*Where* have you got to go?'

Tyler headed for the door, muttering something over his shoulder. Lizzie thought she must have misheard him.

'That sounded like *Robotics Club*,' she muttered to Ethan.

Ethan nodded. 'That's what he said.'

'Robotics? Tyler?' Lizzie shook her head. 'That's impossible. Unless it's got something to do with magic.'

Ethan laughed. '*Magic?*'

Lizzie grinned. 'Not spells and potions. Stuff like card tricks and sawing people in half. That's Tyler's hobby. He wants to be a magician when he grows up.'

'Sounds like fun,' said Ethan. He picked up the broom and started sweeping again.

'It's nice of you to help,' Lizzie said, as she emptied the shovel into the bucket. 'But you don't have to stay. I can manage on my own.'

Ethan stopped sweeping for a moment. 'I'm not just being nice. Actually—I want to talk to you. I was wondering . . .' He hesitated, as if he was working out what to say.

Before he could start again, a loud voice boomed across the canteen. 'Ethan! Why are you hanging around here? You're supposed to be doing circuit training.' It was Mr Wasu, the Head of Sports. He came loping across the canteen and pulled the broom out of Ethan's hands. 'You can't waste time like that. You've got more important things to do!'

Before Ethan could say another word, he was chivvied away, and Lizzie was all on her own. She looked over her shoulder at the little patch of floor they'd cleared and then back at the mess ahead of her. It was no use standing around. She still had a lot of clearing up to do.

It took her three times as long without Tyler and Ethan, but by half past three the canteen was sparkling. And she was exhausted. She hadn't had any lunch and she'd been working flat out for three hours. When Mrs Khan told her she could stop, she had just enough energy to collect her things and stagger to the school gate, to wait for Tyler.

He was tired too. He came trailing out of school with a big bundle of paper in his hands.

'What's that?' Lizzie leaned towards him, trying to see what was on the paper. 'Have you been drawing?'

Tyler's tired face suddenly changed. His eyes stretched wide and a bright grin plastered itself across his face. 'I've been designing a robot!' he said. Almost shouted. 'Look! Isn't it great?' He waved the paper at her.

Lizzie looked down at the top sheet. It was a neat drawing of a complicated humanoid robot. The robot had four arms, two wheels, a screen on its chest, and two cameras for eyes. It looked like the kind of robot Tyler liked drawing when he was seven—except it was much more detailed.

And there were labels all round it, with the measurements written in.

'I've done all the calculations,' Tyler said, in a brisk, business-like voice, 'and put half the circuits together. Tomorrow I'll build the casing and program the control unit—'

'What?' Lizzie's mouth fell open. 'You mean—you're actually *making* this thing?'

'It's called Robo,' Tyler said. 'Robot Operated By Open-source technology. I drew up the spec at lunchtime and I've written most of the computer code already.'

None of that made sense to Lizzie. What did Tyler know about robot design or circuits or computer code? They hadn't even *got* a computer. This Robo thing had to be some kind of game he was playing. She let him babble on about it as they went home. All she could think about making herself a sandwich. As soon as possible.

She clattered up the steps, ahead of Tyler, and unlocked the door. 'Hi Dad!' she called softly. 'Everything OK?'

There was no answer. Her heart gave a thud. *Mum!* she thought. *Something's happened to Mum.* She went straight across the hall and tapped at her parents' bedroom door.

'Mum? Dad? Is everything OK?'.

'Hello darling,' said her mother's voice. 'Come in.'

Lizzie opened the door and there was her mum, sitting up in bed. She looked tired—as usual—but she was smiling.

'How was school?' she said.

'Fine,' Lizzie mumbled. With her fingers crossed behind her back. 'It was all fine.' They weren't supposed to tell Mum anything that might upset her. 'Where's Dad gone?'

Her mother smiled. 'He hasn't gone anywhere. He's in the living room, playing with his new toy.'

'What new toy?' Lizzie said.

'Go and see.' Mum laughed gently. 'They delivered it this morning, from the school. And I've hardly seen him since then.'

Before Lizzie could ask any more, there was a shout from Tyler. He'd gone straight to the living room and he sounded delighted.

'Wowee! That's fantastic, Dad! Where did you get it?'

Mum smiled at Lizzie. 'Tyler likes it too. Go and take a look.'

Lizzie ran across the hall and into the living room. Dad and Tyler were sitting side by side on the sofa, hunched over a computer. And not just any computer. A shiny sky-blue laptop.

Dad looked up and grinned at her. 'Isn't it brilliant? They brought it round from the school this morning. And all those too. Look.'

Lizzie looked. Scattered across the coffee table were half a dozen sky-blue memory sticks with *Hazelbrook* printed on them in neat black letters.

'But why?' she said. 'Why have they given us all this?'

'So the school can keep in touch with me.' Dad nodded at the screen. 'All these wonderful new changes! I've been looking at the website. Can't take my eyes off it.'

'The school website?' Lizzie was amazed. She'd looked at it last year, on one of the school computers, but only once. She'd never been back—because it was totally and utterly boring.

But Dad obviously didn't think so. His eyes were shining and he was grinning all over his face. 'It's a *wonderful* school,' he said again. 'And the Headmaster—

I've watched his message to parents half a dozen times. You two are so *lucky* to be students at Hazelbrook Academy.' He clicked the mouse and beckoned to Lizzie, patting the sofa beside him. 'Come and see!'

Tyler leaned forward eagerly, but Lizzie had had enough of school for one day. 'I'll look later on,' she muttered.

And she went off to the kitchen to make her sandwich.

# 6

# HACKING

Ethan was very tired when he finished circuit training. It took him twice as long as usual to cycle home from school. By the time he got there, Auntie Beryl was back from work. When he let himself in, she was sitting in the living room, with her laptop on her knee. She looked up and beamed at him.

'Ethan, I am *so proud* of you! I've watched the match three times already. You're sensational!'

'Sorry?' Ethan had no idea what she was talking about.

'You have to see it.' She slid along the sofa so he could sit beside her. 'I was just taking a quick look at the school website when I saw your name on the sidebar. And when I clicked—look!'

She turned the laptop sideways and Ethan saw himself, hooking the ball away from Piotr and racing down the pitch. The boys running after him were all taller and heavier and older, but they weren't keeping up. And the players in front didn't stop him either. He jinked past one . . . two . . . three . . . leaving them all looking slow and stupid.

Even he could see it was brilliant play. And it was definitely him. But—*how*? He'd never been any good at football before. But there he was on the screen, playing

LOOK INTO MY EYES

like a superstar.

Auntie Beryl threw her arm round his shoulders and gave him a squeeze. 'You're so modest. You never told me you were a football genius.'

'I'm—' He nearly said—what *had* he nearly said?

Suddenly, it wasn't there any more. His mind was completely empty for a second. And then he found himself saying something completely different.

'I'd better get started on my homework.' He gave Auntie Beryl a pale grin and stood up. 'It's running again—and I don't want to go out in the dark.'

'Off you go then.' Auntie Beryl nodded and patted his arm. 'Now I can see why you have to do so much. You must need to be super-fit to play like that.'

Ethan changed into his running kit, and set off. For the first time, he was actually looking forward to his homework run. Not because of the actual running, but because he needed a chance to think. As he headed down the road, his feet set up a steady rhythm—*left, right, left, right*—and he started making a mental list of all the strange things connected with school.

First: football. How come he was suddenly such a brilliant player? And why couldn't he talk about it? It seemed as though his brain stopped him whenever he tried.

*. . . left, right, left, right . . .*

Second: Lizzie. She'd suddenly started throwing food round the canteen, for no reason—and then looked totally confused, as if she couldn't remember doing it. That was just how he'd felt at the end of the football.

And when he asked her about it, her voice had just died away before she could say anything.

Had that happened to him too?

*. . . left, right, left, right . . .*

Third: it was weird the way Auntie Beryl was so obsessed with the school. She was usually very sensible and down-to-earth. Why did she keep raving about Hazelbrook?

*. . . left, right, left, right . . .*

Were all those things linked? Possibly. But how could he find out if his mind kept going blank? Why couldn't he *talk* to people? If only he could just *see* what was going on! If only there was a secret way to watch . . .

*. . . left, right, left, right . . .*

If he was a fly, it would be easy. He could crawl up the wall of Mrs Maron's office and hear what she said on the phone. He could watch her working on her computer and fly all round the school . . .

*. . . left, right, left, right . . .*

He could watch without being spotted, like—

YES! OF COURSE!! THAT WAS IT!!!

He stopped dead and put a hand over his mouth, to stop himself laughing out loud. Because he'd thought of the perfect solution. And he could start as soon as he'd finished his run—and watched the video he had for homework.

All he had to do was hack into the school admin network.

Two hours later, he was in his room, staring at the admin login box. He had a good start. Miss Wellington was really careless and he'd seen her ID and password half a dozen times. Quickly he typed them in:

**V.Wellington.Geography**

**Icecream123**

That got him into the admin network—but not the interesting bit. All he could see was a lot of dull stuff about booking rooms and preparing for the inspection. Miss Wellington obviously wasn't important enough to see anything else.

So who was? The Headmaster, of course. And—how about Mrs Maron? He might be able to guess her login details. He typed in

**B.Maron.Deputy.Head**

**Icecream123**

But all that got him was **Wrong ID and password.**

It took him three days to crack it. He started with the ID, trying all the possible variations of Mrs Maron's name (*Beata.Maron.Deputy* . . . *B.Maron.Deputy* . . . *B.Maron.PR* . . .) working on them while he was out running and typing them in as soon as he got home. Finally, he hit on the right one. When he typed in

**B.Maron.Deputy.PR**

**Icecream123**

he just got **Wrong password**—which meant the ID was right.

He was halfway there. Now he needed a program that could hack the password. It might take a couple more days, but then he'd be in. He downloaded a password hacker and set it working just as Auntie Beryl called him for tea.

But he didn't need the hacking program after all. As he ate his sausages, he was still thinking about the password. Miss Wellington's had eight letters. She'd probably chosen *Icecream* because it was her favourite food, but most people didn't choose foods. They used family names for their passwords.

That was when he realized.

*Mrs Maron's daughter had an eight-letter name.*

He almost jumped up and ran straight back to his bedroom, but he didn't want Auntie Beryl asking questions. So he forced himself to keep eating, and when he'd finished, he cleared the table and loaded the dishwasher. Because that was what he always did.

The password hacker was still churning away when he got back to his computer. He shut it down and typed in

**Angelika123**

And that was it. He was in! He could still see the folders he'd seen when he logged in as Miss Wellington:

**Timetable**

**Room Bookings**

**Staff Meetings**

**Inspection Preparations**

But now there were others too:

**Staff Records**

 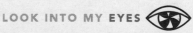

**Finance**

**PMV** (what on earth did that mean?)

And then the thing he was after. Right at the bottom of the list. **Drone Management.**

He took a deep breath and opened the folder.

He was in—but how could he take over a drone without being spotted? It took him a long time to work that out. When Auntie Beryl told him to go to bed, he turned out his light and waited for an hour and a half, until she went to bed herself. Then he started again. It was no use trying to go to sleep until he'd solved it.

It was after midnight when he finally worked it out. He checked all the details, three times, to make sure he was safe. Then he set up the link to his phone and logged out. There was nothing more he could do now.

Not until tomorrow . . .

# 7

# VANDAL!

Lizzie had gone to bed early that night. But when she woke up next morning, she felt exhausted—as if she'd run ten miles, or had nightmares all night.

She was late too. Again. Dad was calling from the kitchen, in a loud, panicky voice. She jumped out of bed and raced into the bathroom, but before she'd even cleaned her teeth, Dad was yelling even louder.

'Lizzie! You'll have to eat your breakfast going up the road! You mustn't be late!'

She ran into her bedroom and started putting on yesterday's clothes. Her shirt was crumpled and a bit grubby, but there was no time to look for anything else. She pulled on her sweatshirt, did up her trousers, and reached for her shoes and socks.

The socks were wet. And the shoes as well.

How come? She didn't remember stepping into any puddles yesterday. There hadn't *been* any to step in. But the socks were certainly wet and cold now. She grabbed a clean pair out of the drawer and pulled them on, but she couldn't do anything about the shoes. She'd just have to go to school with wet feet.

Dad and Tyler were waiting by the front door. Dad pushed a piece of toast into her hand and she and Tyler ran up the road together. Eating and running at the same time was so complicated that she couldn't think about anything except her feet and the toast. But Tyler kept chattering anyway.

'I should finish Robo's computer code today. When I've built his casing. And then—Lizzie! You're not listening.'

Lizzie swallowed a lump of toast as they veered round the corner into the High Street. 'I *am*. But we've got to keep running or we're going to be late. Come on.'

Tyler screeched, raced ahead of her round the next corner—and stopped dead. Lizzie crashed into him and they both fell over.

'Ow!' said Tyler. 'Ow ow ow ow OW!'

'It's your own—'

*It's your own fault*, Lizzie was going to say. But before she could finish, she realized she was wrong. Tyler couldn't help stopping—because the way was blocked by a huge crowd. Half the kids in the school were standing in front of the school gate, staring up at the shiny new notice above it.

Only it didn't look shiny and new any more. It was covered with jagged purple letters, sprayed all over it.

I HATE HAZELBROOK
MRS MARON IS A WITCH

There were splashes of paint everywhere—and more words painted on the pavement and across the playground:

THIS SCHOOL STINKS
WHO NEEDS EDUKCATION?

And that wasn't all. Looking beyond the painted

words, Lizzie saw dark, jagged holes in the school windows. Someone had broken five of them. And smashed one of the glass entrance doors.

Mrs Maron was coming across the playground, picking her way carefully between the splashes of paint. The wind was ruffling her perfect blonde hair and she was flaming with fury.

'No one must touch anything,' she snapped when she reached the gates. 'The police are on their way. And the *inspectors*—' She went bright scarlet. For a second, it looked as if she was going to choke with rage. She took a deep breath and went on. 'Go down to the car park entrance, all of you. You'll have to come in that way. Then go straight to the hall and wait for instructions.'

Lizzie pulled Tyler up and brushed the dust off his coat. There was a smear of paint on his trousers. 'Sorry,' she said. 'I didn't mean to knock you over.'

Tyler hardly heard her. He was staring up at the noticeboard. 'Who did it?' he muttered. 'Who *dared*?'

Lizzie pulled a face. 'Whoever it was, they're going to be in BIG trouble. Come on. We'd better get inside.'

They joined the line of people walking down the pavement and into the car park. Everyone looked tense and upset—which was odd. If this had happened last term, Blake and his friends would have laughed their way into school. They might even have pretended they'd done it, just for a joke.

But no one was laughing now. They all looked shocked and some of the little kids were almost crying. Lizzie heard bits of what people were saying.

' . . . awful thing to do . . .'

' . . . ruining the school's reputation . . .'

'Must be someone from outside.'

'No one from *Hazelbrook* would do anything like that.'

Even Tyler was upset. Lizzie saw his lips tremble as he looked over at the broken windows.

'Don't worry,' she whispered. 'I'm sure they'll mend it all very soon.'

'But suppose they've taken things?' Tyler muttered. 'Suppose they've taken *Robo*!'

No one was going to want a half-built robot, Lizzie thought. But she didn't want to upset Tyler any more, so she just patted his hand as they all filed into the hall. Nobody was talking now. Everyone sat down in silence and stared up at the stage—where there was nothing to see except a big black screen and a row of empty chairs.

Then they heard the unmistakable sound of Mrs Maron's shoes tapping along the corridor. She marched into the hall and up the centre aisle, with a short man and two tall women following her. They were carrying briefcases and looking round at everyone.

'Who are they?' Tyler whispered.

'Must be the inspectors. She said they were coming.' Lizzie shivered. 'Now there's *really* going to be trouble.'

Mrs Maron paused for a second and muttered to Mr Jennings, who was setting up the projector. Then she led the inspectors onto the stage. They all sat down and there was silence again, except for the ticking of the clock at the back of the hall.

For a whole minute, nothing happened. Then, at nine o'clock precisely, everyone stood up. There was total silence—broken by the rustle of a long black gown as a tall, thin figure in dark glasses stalked down the centre of the hall.

The Headmaster.

He walked up onto the stage and turned to look down on them all. It was impossible to tell what he was thinking. The dark glasses hid his eyes and his pale, narrow face was totally expressionless.

'Good morning, everyone,' he said crisply. 'Please sit down.'

They all sank into their seats, gazing up at him. He waited until they were all completely still and then he spoke again.

'Last night, this school was attacked by a criminal hooligan. You have all seen the damage that was done. But there is no need to be alarmed. The person involved is about to be identified. And dealt with.'

He lifted a hand, signalling to Mr Jennings. Immediately, the screen behind him lit up. The Headmaster gave a small, pale smile.

'We have excellent security arrangements,' he said. 'Mr Jennings, please will you play the film from the camera at the front gate.'

He took a step to one side, leaving everyone a clear view of the screen. For a second, Lizzie couldn't make any sense of the dark, fuzzy pictures that appeared. Then she realized that she was looking at a picture of the main school gate, with the big noticeboard above it.

In the foreground was a small, blurred figure, creeping towards the gate.

The figure bent down, picking something up from the ground. Lifting one arm, it held the object high, pointing it at the noticeboard. Then it began to wave it up and down and across.

'Spray-painting,' someone whispered, just behind Lizzie.

The spraying went on for two or three minutes, first on to the noticeboard and then across the ground. Then the dark figure put the can down and started climbing over the gate. The Headmaster gave another thin-lipped smile.

'Now—the pictures from the front door camera,' he said.

The picture changed. Suddenly the dark figure was moving towards the camera. Bending down, it started picking up things from the ground, cradling them in one arm. Then it threw them at the building, very quickly—one, two, three, four, five. There was a sound of breaking glass. The fire alarm started ringing and all the security lights came on.

They shone straight on to the vandal's face.

The Headmaster nodded at Mr Jennings to pause the film and zoom in. There was a gasp from everyone in the hall and the people around Lizzie turned to look at her.

She stared at the picture in horror. 'No!' she said. 'No—that's . . . that's impossible! I didn't—'

And then her voice faded away.

# 8

# DRONE NO.4

When Ethan heard Lizzie's voice, he turned round to look—and he saw the moment when her expression changed. For a second, she was staring up at the picture on the screen, looking amazed and disbelieving. And then—nothing. Her voice cut out, her eyes stopped focussing, and her face went totally blank.

That was exactly what happened to him. It had to be the same thing.

She'd done the spray-painting all right. And broken the windows. There was no mistaking the face on the screen, with its mass of curly hair. But she didn't seem to remember anything about it. And why hadn't she worn a scarf or a balaclava? She'd looked straight up at the camera—almost as if she *wanted* to be seen.

The Headmaster was watching her too. 'Come up here,' he said crisply. He nodded to Mr Jennings. 'Play the film again.'

The fuzzy images flickered across the screen. The hall was completely silent except for the sound of Lizzie scrambling to her feet and stumbling down the centre of the hall. As she walked up the steps on to the stage, the Headmaster pointed at her with one pale finger, looking round at the three inspectors behind him.

'This is what we have to work with,' he said.

'Children like this are our raw material. Last term, this girl was almost excluded, for attacking another student. Having missed the first part of this term, she came back yesterday—expecting to find herself in the same lawless, chaotic school as before. Now her violence has turned against the school itself.'

The inspectors stared at Lizzie, shaking their heads. Ethan could see what they were thinking. *Disgraceful! Absolutely disgraceful!*

Lizzie looked frightened and nervous, but her real face was dwarfed by the image on the screen behind her—the face of a fierce, curly-headed vandal, looking exultantly at the school's broken windows. The Headmaster was silent for a moment, giving everyone time to absorb the picture. Then he spoke to the inspectors again—and his voice was steely and determined.

'Pupils like this are a challenge. But we can meet that challenge. Come back in a few weeks and you will find this girl transformed. She will have been moulded into a docile, obedient pupil, with a skill that will make her useful for the rest of her life. Because, at Hazelbrook Academy—' he turned to look down the hall, and the whole school finished his sentence '—every student is a star!'

Ethan found himself saying the words with everyone else. Even Lizzie's little brother was saying them. And the inspectors were beaming down the hall, as if they couldn't wait to write a brilliant report.

What should have been a disastrous inspection was

turning into a triumph.

The Headmaster turned to Lizzie. 'Other schools would turn you over to the police,' he said icily. 'But at this school we recognize children as they are—grubby, talentless, and uncivilized—and we transform them into the people our country needs. Mrs Maron?'

'Yes, Headmaster?' She stepped forward briskly from the back of the stage.

'I shall take the inspectors to my office, to discuss their report. When we have left, please tell the police I will deal with this myself. Then dismiss the students and send this girl to my office.'

'Yes, Headmaster!' Mrs Maron said brightly.

The Headmaster led the three inspectors off the stage and away down the hall, leaving Lizzie standing on her own, facing the rest of the school.

*I need to talk to her*, Ethan thought. *I really need to talk to her*. He couldn't march onto the stage in front of the whole school, though. He needed to get her on her own.

But, even then, how could they talk if their minds kept going blank? If only he understood a bit more about what was going on! The Headmaster was right at the centre of things—he was sure of that. He wished he could see what happened when Lizzie went to the Headmaster's office. If only . . .

But he could! What an idiot he was. Of *course* he could.

When Mrs Maron dismissed them, he was the first person out of the hall. He hurried to the changing rooms, going as fast as he could go without running. All he needed was a few moments by himself, to set up his drone. And there was one place where no one else would go, first thing in the morning.

The showers.

By the time he reached the boys' changing room, he was so far ahead of everyone else that no one saw him dart through the door of the showers. He already had his phone in his hand and in a few seconds he had logged on and opened up the *Drone Management* folder.

Drone No. 4 was the one he'd taken over last night. He set it to replay yesterday's film on the school system—no one would ever notice the difference—and then worked out what he actually wanted it to do.

He couldn't send it right into the Headmaster's office. It was sure to be spotted there. But it might not be noticed if it was outside the window. He might just get away with that.

Already he could hear other people coming into the changing room. There was no time for second thoughts. Calling up the plan of the school, he worked out a route and programmed it into the drone. Then he logged off, as fast as he could, and pushed the phone into his pocket.

Now all he had to do was explain why he'd been in the showers.

He took off one of his shoes and removed a sock. Then he put on the shoe again and dropped the sock into a puddle of greyish water under the shower. When he picked it up, it looked as though it had been soaking there all night. Wet and disgusting.

Racing out into the changing room, he waved the sock over his head. 'Got it!' he shouted. 'Phew!'

'Got what?' Stan, the goalie, looked across and pulled a face. 'Yee-*uck!* If that was my sock, I'd have left it there.'

'My Auntie Beryl would kill me,' Ethan said, thinking, *Sorry, Auntie Beryl.* 'She goes crazy if I lose my clothes.'

'You live with your *aunt*?' Stan said.

Ethan did the explanation about his parents being anthropologists in the South American jungle. 'They're only home in the summer holidays. So I live with Auntie Beryl the rest of the time.'

'And she nags you about *socks*?' That was Piotr. He shook his head. 'Adults—totally weird.'

'What's that? What's that?' Mr Wasu came bursting into the changing room. 'I don't want any chat except about football! You need to focus, boys. *Focus!*'

That was so funny that Ethan almost laughed. He knew he wouldn't be focussing on anything. For the next two hours they'd be out on the field—and his mind would be a complete blank.

But Lizzie would be in the Headmaster's office, for some of the time at least.

What was going on there?

# 9
# ROBOT

Twenty minutes later, Lizzie was just coming round, blinking at the empty space in front of her. She was standing in the Headmaster's office and she was sure something had just happened. But what?

All she could remember was walking into the room and finding no one there. Then the air in front of her had started glittering. And after that?

She had no idea what had happened.

All she knew was that she had to go to the information hub. Straight away.

The idea came into her head quite suddenly, out of nowhere. Before she could wonder how—or work out what the information hub was—her feet started moving towards the door. She found herself walking out of the room and up the stairs that led to the library.

But it wasn't a library any more. There was a new notice on the door. It said: *Information hub: ring and ask for admission*. The door was shut tightly and there was an electric bell on the wall.

She pressed the bell and two seconds later the door flew open. There was Mr Bains, the librarian—but where was his beard? And why was he wearing a suit and tie instead of one of his lovely bright sweaters?

'H-hello,' Lizzie faltered.

'Good morning,' Mr Bains said solemnly. He looked down at the tablet in his hand. 'Ah yes, I was expecting you. Come in, Lizzie.' He waved her into the room. 'Everything's ready for you.'

Lizzie stepped inside and looked around. It was a long room on the first floor, with big windows and solid glass walls. Once it had been crammed with books. Shelves and shelves of them. Now there was only one bookcase, down at the far end, and the rest of the room was filled with computer screens and shelves of magazines and files.

'Where are all the books?' she said.

'Technology has moved on.' Mr Bains's voice sounded odd, as if he was reciting something. 'Very few books are necessary to access information now. I have put the one you need on that table over there.'

He waved her across the room and she sat down at the table, feeling as if she'd wandered into some strange dream. Had Mr Bains just said that books were unnecessary? *Mr Bains?*

She felt even odder when she looked down at what he'd laid out for her. Next to the computer terminal, there was a small, battered book which said 'Shakespeare's Sonnets' on the cover. Next to it was a list of websites with names like www.Shakespeare.grammar.com and www.grammaranalysis.com/Shakespeare.

What was she supposed to do with those?

Before she could even think about it, she found herself sitting down at the computer and logging on. Her fingers started moving over the keyboard, opening a new document and typing in a heading: 'Imagery and Grammatical Structures in Shakespeare's Sonnet Number 18'.

She didn't understand what it meant. But then she didn't even know she was doing it.

Her mind was completely empty.

The next thing she knew, the bell was ringing for lunch. She lifted her hands off the keyboard and a message blinked at her: *LOG OUT NOW*. She clicked on it and stood up, stretching because she felt so stiff.

As she walked towards the door, Mr Bains gave her an odd little smile. He looked . . . sad. 'That sonnet is my favourite poem,' he said. 'Don't you think it's beautiful?'

'The sonnet?' Lizzie said. 'I didn't—'

*Didn't what?* She had no idea what she'd been going to say. She gave Mr Bains a feeble smile. 'It's very . . . interesting,' she muttered.

Mr Bains looked puzzled, but he didn't say anything else. He just opened the door to let her out and watched her walk away down the corridor.

Lizzie headed for the canteen. She was hoping to meet Tyler, but she didn't know how she was going to spot him. There was a huge crowd of people in the doorway, all laughing and chattering and standing on tiptoe to try and see over each other's heads. They seemed to be staring at something really interesting inside the canteen.

When she reached the edge of the crowd, she heard Angelika's voice, shouting above all the chattering. 'Send it over here, Tyler! Tell it to say, "Angelika has great coffee!" '

Lizzie started pushing her way through the crowd. It was easier than she expected. When people looked round and saw who it was, they shrank away from her. 'It's the vandal,' she heard someone whisper. In a few seconds, she found herself right at the front.

And there was Tyler, standing beside the lunch counter, looking proud and embarrassed. Next to him was a tall shiny robot with four arms, two wheels, a screen on its chest, and two cameras for eyes.

Tyler had a remote control in his hand and he was tapping at the buttons as fast as he could. Suddenly, the robot's wheels started to spin. It zoomed across the floor, screeched to a stop in front of Angelika's coffee stall, and squeaked: 'GET YOUR ANGELIC COFFEE HERE! AND GREAT HOT CHOCOLATE!'

Everyone laughed and cheered, and several people went across and ordered hot drinks. But Tyler was staring at the robot with a strange expression on his face. Lizzie fought her way across to him.

'What's the matter, Ty? They all think you're brilliant.'

'But I didn't—' Tyler said. And then he just . . . stopped. His eyes wandered away from Lizzie, as if he couldn't really see her.

'Yes, you *did*!' Lizzie said. 'You drew that robot—and now you've made it. It's sensational.'

Tyler bit his lip and looked down at the floor. Lizzie thought he was going to say something else, but before he could speak, Mrs Maron came sweeping into the canteen. She clapped her hands and called over the heads of the crowd.

'Stop pushing each other. Let's have a proper line to the counter. Come on, now. And don't swamp Angelika's stall.'

People shuffled back obediently, and Mrs Maron saw the robot standing in front of the coffee stall.

'What's that doing there?' she said sharply.

Angelika beamed at her. 'It's been advertising my coffee.' She looked at Tyler. 'Do it again, so my mum can hear.'

Nervously, Tyler prodded at the remote control. Over on the other side of the canteen, the robot lifted its head and spoke again: 'DON'T MISS ANGELIKA'S AMAZING HOT DRINKS. DELICIOUS COFFEE AND SPECIAL HOT CHOCOLATE.'

Mrs Maron looked delighted. 'That's brilliant!' she said. 'A really clever piece of advertising.'

'Maybe the robot could do other things too,' Angelika said. 'Like . . . whipping the cream or grating the chocolate.'

Tyler had made a robot that could *whip cream*? That sounded impossible to Lizzie, but Mrs Maron was delighted. She almost hugged Angelika. 'There's your breakthrough idea! A chain of coffee shops with robot staff. That would be unique—and cheaper than employing real people.'

'It's Tyler's robot,' Angelika said.

'Then you need to talk to him.' Mrs Maron smiled at Tyler across the canteen. 'You and Angelika ought to schedule a proper business meeting.'

Tyler looked terrified.

'Maybe . . . another day?' Lizzie said quickly.

Mrs Maron's smile disappeared. She looked severely at Lizzie. 'You should be glad that *someone* in your family is doing something useful,' she said. And she turned round and swept out of the canteen.

Lots of other people were glaring at Lizzie too. She ate her dinner as fast as she could and hurried back to the information hub. As she sat down in front of the computer again, she was almost looking forward to the moment when her mind went blank.

It seemed like a very long time to the end of the day. And she was longing to go home.

But when she got home, things were even worse. As she and Tyler walked into the flat, Lizzie heard the sounds coming from the computer and she knew Dad was on the school website.

'*Come back in a few weeks,*' the Headmaster's voice was saying, '*and you will find this girl transformed. She will have been moulded into a docile, obedient pupil . . .*'

When Dad saw her, he looked as if he was going to burst into tears. 'How *could* you?' he said. 'All that trouble last term was bad enough. But this—'

Lizzie ran over to look at the screen. There—posted up for all the world to see—was a still from the Headmaster's video. A figure caught in the security light, about to throw a rock through the school window. The face was blanked out, but the hair and the sweatshirt were unmistakable. It was obviously her.

'He can't do that!' she said. 'He can't put me on the internet like that!'

Dad shook his head. 'It's for your own good,' he said sadly. 'They phoned up and told me all about it this afternoon. Just be glad the Headmaster didn't throw you out of the school.'

'That's not fair!' Lizzie said. 'I wasn't—'

Wasn't—what? Suddenly, she couldn't remember.

'Liz?' her mother called from the bedroom. 'Is that you?'

'Don't upset Mum!' Dad hissed. 'I haven't told her about all this. Not a word!'

Lizzie nodded, feeling too sick to speak. Then she went across the hall into her parents' bedroom. Her mother was in bed, as usual propped up with half a dozen pillows.

'Come and tell me what's wrong,' she said.

Lizzie perched on the edge of the bed, wondering what to say. Last term, when she'd had the fight with Blake, her mother had been seriously ill. And hearing about the fight had made her worse. Now she was getting better, it would be terrible to upset her again.

'It's nothing,' Lizzie muttered, looking down. 'I've just got a headache.'

There was a little pause. Then her mother said, 'Is everything . . . all right at school?'

'It's fine,' Lizzie said quickly. 'Absolutely fine.'

'No trouble with that boy Blake?'

Lizzie shook her head.

There was another pause. Then her mother said very carefully, 'Dad says things are . . . different at school this term. Is that right? He keeps looking at the school website and he seems very excited about it all.'

'Yes,' Lizzie muttered.

Her mother waited for a moment, as if she was expecting a bit more. Then she patted Lizzie's hand. 'So what did you do at school today?'

Before she had time to think, Lizzie found words flooding out of her mouth. 'It was wonderful. I spent the morning studying grammar and imagery in one of Shakespeare's sonnets. And in the afternoon I plotted my results on a series of graphs.'

Her mother blinked. 'And did you—*enjoy* all that?'

'It was intellectually stimulating,' Lizzie heard herself say.

'That sounds . . . good,' her mother said slowly, watching Lizzie's face. 'And are you *happy* there, Liz?'

Lizzie felt her mouth twist into a wide, bright smile. 'Hazelbrook Academy is a brilliant school,' she gushed. 'It's helped me discover my true skills and my real ambition.'

Her mother didn't smile back. *She knows something's wrong,* Lizzie thought. *I've got to go away or she'll start worrying.*

She stood up quickly. 'I'd better go and start my homework. Shall I fetch you a drink?'

'Not just now,' her mother said faintly. 'I think I'll have a little sleep.'

She closed her eyes and Lizzie tiptoed out of the room, boiling with frustration. It was bad enough not being able to tell her mother about not remembering the vandalism. But she'd done more than that. What had made her say all that rubbish about how wonderful the school was?

*I don't understand*, she thought. *What's happening to me?*

When she looked into the living room, Dad was still hunched over the computer. She nodded at Tyler. 'Come into the kitchen and I'll make us a cup of tea.'

Tyler padded after her, looking worried and miserable. 'Dad asked me about school,' he said unhappily. 'And I told him—' Before he could go on, his mouth twisted itself into a bright, artificial smile.

'It's OK,' Lizzie said quickly. 'I know what you said.' She put the kettle on and then she turned round and smiled at him. 'Why don't you do something you really like? Practise one of your magic tricks.'

Tyler's smile didn't change. 'There is no such thing as magic,' he said, in a brisk, mechanical voice. 'Nothing is worth studying except robotics and computer technology. I have three hours' homework to do, updating Robo's software.'

'For goodness' sake!' Lizzie said. She ran across to his bedroom and fetched his favourite pack of cards.

'Here you are,' she said as she ran back into the kitchen. 'Don't try and talk. Just have some *fun*.'

She put the cards down on the table and Tyler stared at them for a moment. Then he smiled. He sat down and started shuffling the cards so quickly she could hardly see his hands.

## 10

# WHAT THE DRONE SAW

Ethan was sitting in his bedroom, logging on to the school network. As soon as he was in, he opened the *Drone Management* folder and found the files from the drone he'd hijacked.

Had it filmed anything useful?

It had been too risky to try and look on his phone, at school, And, even now he was at home, he felt so nervous that his hands were shaking. He fast-forwarded through the film until he reached the right time and paused it when he saw the window of the Headmaster's office.

The picture was perfect, just as he'd hoped. The drone was hovering just outside the window, opposite the office door. Ethan started the film playing again and saw the door opening and Lizzie walking into the room.

But—the Headmaster wasn't there.

Ethan frowned. That didn't make sense. Lizzie wouldn't have gone in without being called. So where was the Headmaster?

Lizzie looked just as baffled as Ethan felt. But only for a few seconds. Then, in the middle of the room, the air began to sparkle and shiver, like a cloud of tiny, silvery midges. At first, it was just a strange, formless shimmering. But gradually, it thickened and a tall, figure began to take shape.

Ethan saw Lizzie open her mouth, as if she was going to speak. But she didn't say anything. She just stared as the Headmaster appeared in front of her, with one hand raised to take off his dark glasses.

For an instant, as the glasses came off, Ethan saw the Headmaster's pale, luminous eyes. *I've seen them before*, he thought. *When I was in his office. He looked at me, just like that, and he said . . . he said . . . What was it?* He couldn't remember.

On the film, the Headmaster opened his mouth. In the split second before he started speaking, Ethan realized what he had to do. If he went on looking at the film, he might forget all this as well. He closed his eyes tight, covering them with his hands to block out every glimmer of light from the Headmaster's pale, compelling eyes. He didn't see any more of the film.

But he heard what the Headmaster said to Lizzie. Every single word of it. And suddenly, all the strange things about Hazelbrook Academy started making sense.

Terrible, dangerous sense.

What was he going to do about it?

He spent the whole weekend thinking. He had to tell Lizzie what he'd found out, but he couldn't do that at school. They needed to meet somewhere safe, away from the drones. Only—how was he going to arrange that, when he didn't know her phone number or where she lived? Writing a note was too risky. She might drop it, or show it to someone else. No, he'd have to speak to her—being very careful where he did it.

While they were sitting in registration on Wednesday, he worked out a plan. When they all stood up to leave, he made sure he was right behind her. She turned left, towards the information hub, and he took a couple of quick steps, to catch up. Out of the corner of his eye, he could see a drone hovering right above them. It wasn't his.

'Hi, Lizzie,' he said, trying to sound casual. 'What have you got now?'

She gave him the wide, plastic smile he was expecting. 'I'll be writing a report on Shakespeare's grammar,' she said. As if that was the best thing in the world.

Ethan managed to look surprised. 'How do you know about that?' he said. 'Is it interesting?' He started to walk a little faster, to get ahead of the drone.

'It's the most interesting thing I've ever done,' Lizzie said, still in the same keen, artificial voice. 'I'm so grateful to Hazelbrook Academy for helping me discover my true skills and interests . . .'

Ethan let her go on talking until they were almost at the left turn that led to the changing rooms. By then, they were about twenty metres ahead of the drone. As they reached the corner, he interrupted her.

'I need to talk to you,' he muttered. 'Something important—about school.'

He turned left, towards the changing rooms, looking

over his shoulder to see if Lizzie would follow. She hesitated for a moment and then came after him.

'OK, what's so important?' she said warily.

'I've got something to tell you. But not here.' Ethan looked past her, making sure the drone hadn't reached the corner. 'Can you meet me after school? In the park?'

For a second, Lizzie was too surprised to speak. Ethan was still waiting for her answer when he saw the drone going past the end of the corridor. They'd almost run out of time.

'It's *really* important,' he muttered. 'Come if you can. I'll wait behind the bandstand.'

Over Lizzie's shoulder, he saw the drone drifting back again. And this time it turned the corner, heading straight towards them. Lizzie hadn't seen it, because she was facing the other way. If he tried to warn her, that might look suspicious.

But if he didn't warn her, she might say something dangerous.

There was only one safe thing to do. He turned away and walked off to the changing room, without saying a word. With any luck, Lizzie would understand when she turned round and saw the drone. If she didn't, he'd have to explain when they met after school.

If she came.

 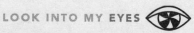

# 11

# SECRET MEETING

What was all that about? Lizzie didn't know what to think. She stood and watched Ethan disappear into the changing room. Then she turned to go.

And that was when she saw the drone.

Was that why Ethan had left so suddenly? Was he afraid the drone would spot them together? Why did that matter? A little shiver went down her back. It all felt like trouble—and she'd had enough trouble for one term.

She could feel herself trembling as she headed for the information hub. Whatever Ethan wanted, she wasn't going to get mixed up in it. If he went to the park after school, he would be on his own.

But at lunchtime something changed her mind.

As she went into the canteen, she could see people staring at her. When she walked up to the food counter, they edged away as if they thought she might start throwing food again. She bought her lunch, as quickly as she could, and turned round to look for a seat.

But her feet had other ideas. Instead of heading for a table, they took her across the canteen, to Angelika's coffee stall. All Angelika's drinks were much too expensive for her, but she found herself joining the queue. And when she reached the front, she started speaking.

'Hot chocolate, please, with marshmallows and cream.'

'That's what everyone wants today,' Angelika said brightly. 'It's almost as if they've been told what to order. Luckily, I've got *just* enough marshmallows.'

'Almost as if you've been told what to order,' Lizzie said.

She'd meant it as a joke, but Angelika gave her a suspicious look. '*Did* someone tell you to order hot chocolate? You've never bought anything here before.'

Lizzie started to shake her head. Then she thought, *Maybe someone did. Is that possible?* There was something odd about the way she'd suddenly wanted hot chocolate. And—oh goodness—what about the money? She emptied her purse into her hand and started counting quickly.

There was just enough there. She would have to use tomorrow's lunch money—but what could she do? The hot chocolate was already there, on the counter, and she'd certainly asked for it. She handed the coins to Angelika and lifted the mug on to her tray.

When she looked up, Angelika was watching her, with an odd expression on her face. 'Here!' she said, holding out the coins. 'Have this one on me.'

'That's very nice of you,' Lizzie said carefully. 'But I can't—I mean—why?'

Angelika went red. 'I've made loads of money today,'

she muttered. 'It's embarrassing how much. And that was everything in your purse, wasn't it?' She dropped the coins on to the counter. 'I'd like to treat you.'

Lizzie picked the money up, feeling awkward and embarrassed. 'That's very kind—especially after I messed up your stall the other day. I really didn't mean—'

Didn't mean—what? She had no idea any more.

'I was wondering about that,' Angelika said slowly. 'Everyone said it was weird, because you'd always been very quiet before. Except when you had a fight with Blake, and they all knew that was his fault. People keep saying it's funny how you've . . . *changed* since last term.'

'Everything's changed since last term,' Lizzie said carefully.

'I just wondered . . .' Angelika lowered her voice. 'My mum's never worked in a school before. The Headmaster wanted someone who'd worked in public relations and Mum said it was a really good job. But—'

'But what?' Lizzie said.

'But *she's* changed.' Angelika stopped, as if she was hunting for the right words. 'She keeps doing things that . . . that aren't like her. And she keeps *smiling*, like . . . like—'

'I know that smile,' Lizzie said slowly. She was thinking of Dad, when he talked about Hazelbrook. And Blake, when he'd welcomed them into the school. That was strange too.

It would be good to talk about all that. But she could

see a drone coming towards them. And anyway, if there *was* something odd going on, was it sensible to talk to *Angelika*? The Deputy Head's daughter.

She shivered and moved away from the counter. 'Don't worry,' she said. 'I expect your mum's just tired. It's a new job and she must be working really hard. Thanks for the hot chocolate.' Giving Angelika a friendly smile, she went off to find a seat.

But the conversation started her thinking. *She'd* changed all right—or she wouldn't have been studying Shakespeare's grammar. And it sounded as though Mrs Maron had changed too. But they weren't the only ones. What about Tyler—who'd stopped doing magic tricks and started building electronic robots?

And Blake, who'd changed from a thuggish bully into a super-polite welcomer?

And maybe Angelika too. She kept talking about building up a huge catering empire—but she seemed to be embarrassed about making lots of money.

That was a lot of changes.

Lizzie puzzled over it all as she ate her lunch. But there was too much to think about. It went round and round in her head, until she felt her brain was going to explode. She needed someone to *talk* to. Someone she could trust, who would help her make sense of what was happening.

Someone like—Ethan? Was he wondering about the same things as she was? She had no idea what he wanted to tell her, but it might be worth finding out.

Maybe she would go to the park after all . . .

She wasn't going to take Tyler. When she met him, on her way out of lunch, she said, 'I've got something to do after school, so you'd better go home on your own. Right?'

She tried to sound offhand, as if it was nothing important, but Tyler gave her an anxious look.

'*What* have you got to do?'

'Nothing special,' Lizzie said vaguely. 'I'm just going to . . . meet someone.'

Tyler looked even more anxious. 'You're not going to do anything . . . *weird*, are you? If you get into trouble again—' He stopped short.

For a second, Lizzie thought he was going to burst into tears. She could see he was really worried and she wanted to explain. But there were a couple of drones hanging around, close enough to pick up anything she said.

She had to do something. Quickly. 'It's nothing weird,' she said, giving Tyler a grin. 'You can come along too, if you like. OK?'

Tyler hesitated and then nodded. 'OK,' he muttered. But he was frowning as he went off along the corridor, as if he was still worrying.

Lizzie watched him go, hoping she'd made the right decision.

She was planning to slip out of school very quietly at the end of the day. So no one noticed that she and Tyler weren't heading home. She wasn't expecting Robo.

When Tyler turned up at the gate, the robot was rolling along beside him. With a crowd of other kids following, asking excited questions.

'Can you make him dance, Ty?'

'Could he beat the world chess champion?'

'Can he speak French?'

It was chaos. Lizzie was almost relieved when Mrs Maron came out of the main entrance. She obviously didn't like seeing a mob of people milling round the gate.

'You're spoiling the school's image,' she said. 'The buses are waiting—and I'm sure you're all keen to go home and start your homework.'

There was an explosion of super-bright smiles. 'Yay!' said half a dozen voices and most people headed off towards the car park.

Mrs Maron frowned at Robo. 'Have you got permission to take that robot out of the building?'

Tyler nodded and took a bundle of papers out of his bag. 'I need him for my homework. Look. I have to get him to collect some data and then do this bit of programming and then—'

'All right, all right.' Mrs Maron flapped her hand at him. 'Then you'd better go home and get started, hadn't you?'

Tyler gave her a wide, enthusiastic grin. 'We're going for a walk first. Robo's going to collect the data with his cameras.' He and Robo went through the gate and set off down the road.

'I was really clever, wasn't I?' Tyler said, when Lizzie caught them up. 'Now no one will wonder why we're not going straight home. Robo's really useful.'

'I still wish you hadn't brought him,' Lizzie said. 'He's so . . . *noticeable*.'

'I couldn't leave him behind,' Tyler said. 'He might have been upset.'

'Tyler—he's a *robot*. And you're supposed to be a computer engineer. That's not how engineers talk about machines.'

'I'm not an engineer,' Tyler muttered. 'I'm a *magician*. I don't even like—' His voice drifted off into silence.

'Ty?' Lizzie said. She caught hold of his hand and shook it. 'Are you all right?'

'What?' Tyler blinked. And then grinned at her, as if he couldn't remember what he'd been talking about. 'Course I am. Where are we going?'

'We're going to the park,' Lizzie said. 'To meet Ethan. I'm not quite sure what he wants, but I need to talk to him. Come on.'

They marched off, with Robo trundling along beside them, and headed into the park and across the grass. For a moment, it looked as though there was no one waiting behind the bandstand. Then Lizzie spotted a pair of feet in the bushes.

'Hi,' she said. 'Is that you, Ethan?'

'Hello.' Ethan's head appeared between two rhododendron bushes. 'Oh,' he said, when he saw Tyler.

'Sorry,' Lizzie said. 'He made such a fuss I had to

bring him. And he wouldn't leave his robot behind.'

'Robot?' Ethan hadn't spotted Robo. When he did, he gave him a long, careful look and then he grinned. 'Actually, I think the robot could be useful,' he said. 'Can you get him in here, where no one's going to see us?'

How could Robo be useful? Lizzie had no idea, but she held the rhododendron branches out of the way while Tyler steered him into the shadows. In the middle of the thicket, there was a dark, empty space and, when they were all there, Ethan took out his phone and held it up.

'I've got something to show you,' he said softly. 'Footage from one of the school drones. Can we play it on your robot, Tyler? So we can all see at once.'

Tyler looked amazed. 'Can Robo do that?'

'I just have to put my phone into the docking station. . . here.' Ethan pushed the phone into a slot just below Robo's screen. Then he tapped the controls above it. 'Ready? OK, this is you, Lizzie, in the Headmaster's office.'

'**Video starting,**' said Robo's creaky voice. His screen lit up—and there was a picture of Lizzie, in the middle of his chest.

'How on earth did you get *that*?' Lizzie said.

'Shh!' whispered Ethan. 'Just watch.'

Lizzie saw herself gazing round the Headmaster's empty office. After a few seconds, the air in the middle of the office started to sparkle and shiver. And then, gradually, out of nothing, a shape began to appear.

Tyler gasped in amazement. 'What's happening?'

'Shh,' whispered Ethan. 'It's a hologram. But you mustn't go on looking at it, or you might forget everything. Get ready to shut your eyes when he takes off his glasses.'

For a moment, Lizzie didn't understand. Then the shimmering shape on the screen began to grow steadier and thicker. And suddenly, she knew what she was looking at.

'It's him!' she said. 'It's the Headmaster!'

She saw herself on the screen, turning to face the dark figure. And then his hand went up towards his glasses.

'Now!' Ethan whispered urgently. 'Shut your eyes *now*!'

For an instant, Lizzie saw the Headmaster's eyes staring, cold and green, out of Robo's chest. Then she closed her eyes tight. But she could still hear his voice. It was very faint, muffled by the window in between him and the drone, but the words were clear.

'Look at me.'

Even though it was just a video, she had to struggle to keep her eyes shut. She clapped her hands over them and listened harder.

'You are very sleepy,' the Headmaster murmured. 'Too sleepy to think for yourself. You can feel yourself drifting away. Drifting slowly away . . .'

Even with her eyes covered, Lizzie found it hard to concentrate. She felt her thoughts begin to dissolve as the Headmaster's voice went on speaking. As if her mind was floating away . . .

Ethan tapped her hard on the back of her hand. 'Don't let him get to you. You mustn't miss the next bit, or you'll never understand what he's doing.'

With an effort, Lizzie dragged her mind out of the mist that had drifted over it. As she did, the Headmaster's voice changed. Suddenly, it was cold and hard.

'Listen carefully,' it said. 'I am going to give you important instructions. When I have finished speaking, you will leave this room and go directly to the information hub. You will not consciously remember anything that has happened in here, but you will follow the instructions, exactly and precisely. When you reach the information hub, the Resources Manager will have everything ready for you. You will log on—'

He went on speaking for almost ten minutes, describing what Lizzie had to do in the information hub, and how she must reply to people who asked about her work.

And then his voice sharpened. 'You will not be able to say anything negative about this, or talk about what I have ordered you to forget. If you try, your mind will simply stop working, until you think about something else. Like this.'

*Like what?* Lizzie's eyes opened, before she could stop them. And she saw herself on the screen, looking vacant and unfocussed, with her eyes wide and her mouth half open.

Exactly like Tyler, a few minutes before.

The hologram was already dissolving. The

 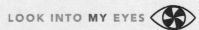

Headmaster vanished, in front of their eyes, and they could see Lizzie on her own again, in the empty room. She looked round for a second, blinking, as if she'd just woken up. Then she turned and went out, closing the door behind her.

Ethan reached forward and pulled his phone out of the docking station. 'This is serious stuff,' he said. 'We need to talk.'

Lizzie was still staring at the blank screen. 'Was all that *real*?' she said shakily.

'All of it,' Ethan said. 'I wanted to know why the school's so strange, so I hacked into the admin system and took over one of the drones.'

'But why me?' Lizzie said. 'Why did you get it to track me?'

'Because of the way you looked when you saw that film from the security camera—with the graffiti and the broken windows. At the end, when we saw your face, you were really amazed. I could tell. You'd done all that stuff—*but you didn't know you had.*'

'That doesn't make sense,' Tyler said. 'How could she *not* know?'

'Because she was hypnotized.' Ethan looked at them both. 'That's what the Headmaster does. He *hypnotizes* people.'

'You mean—' Lizzie began.

But she never finished what she was saying. Because there was a strange noise from the far side of the bandstand. A peculiar, half-strangled noise. Like a muffled sob.

'There's someone there!' Tyler said. 'Someone's listening to us!'

 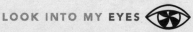

# 12

# ANGELIKA

Ethan moved while the other two were still staring. He shot past them, out of the bushes and round the bandstand. And there was Angelika, crouching down with her hands over her face.

He grabbed her arm, to stop her running away. 'What are you doing?' he said. 'Why were you snooping!'

'I wasn't snooping! You don't understand!' Angelika tried to tug her arm free. 'I just wanted to talk to Lizzie. Because she understood about my mum and the horrible smile. So I followed her into the park. But when I got to the bandstand, I didn't know where she'd gone. Until I heard you talking in the bushes. And then you started playing the film—'

'And you heard everything,' Ethan said. 'Right?'

Angelika nodded. 'I didn't want to spy on you. But I was afraid you'd spot me if I tried to leave. So I just kept still. And I heard . . . I heard—' Her voice started shaking and she put her hands over her mouth.

Lizzie and Tyler came out of the bushes with Robo behind them. Lizzie took one look at Angelika and put an arm round her shoulders. 'Let her go, Ethan.'

Ethan hesitated for a second. Then he dropped Angelika's arm.

She looked up at him. 'I'm sure my mum's been

hypnotized, like Lizzie. And maybe I have too. I keep saying I love the coffee stall, but I don't really—' She broke off and gazed round vaguely.

Ethan and Lizzie looked at each other. Was that real? Or was she pretending?

'Don't talk about yourself,' Ethan said. 'Talk about—talk about someone else.'

Angelika frowned. 'I don't understand. What do you mean?'

Ethan turned and looked at Robo. 'OK, Tyler. Did you build this robot?'

Tyler's mouth stretched into a wide, artificial smile. 'Yes, I did,' he said enthusiastically. 'I *love* electronics, so I designed the robot and wrote all the code and built the circuits and—'

'That's enough.' Ethan held up a hand to stop him. 'Now let me say what *actually* happened. You obviously *didn't* design the robot. You didn't even know he had that docking slot until I used it just now. When you were in the computer engineering room, your mind went completely blank. When you woke up, there was the robot. And everyone was telling you how clever you were to make him.'

Tyler's mouth dropped open. 'How did you *know*?'

Ethan grinned. 'Because I'm a brilliant footballer,' he said. He turned his head and looked at Angelika.

She frowned for a second. And then she grinned back at him. 'Right! You're *not* a brilliant footballer, are you? You were probably rubbish until the Headmaster hypnotized you. Now everyone's telling you you're a superstar, but you can't remember anything about the games you play. And I bet you hate football.'

'But what about me?' Lizzie said. 'Why would the Headmaster make me vandalize the school? And throw food round the canteen?'

Ethan had been thinking about that. 'I think he did it because the inspectors were coming,' he said.

Tyler frowned. 'That doesn't make sense.'

'Yes, it does,' Ethan said. 'Remember what he said when Lizzie went up on the stage? *Pupils like this are a challenge. But we can meet that challenge. Come back in a few weeks and you will find this girl transformed. She will have been moulded into a docile, obedient pupil, with a skill that will make her useful for the rest of her life.'*

Lizzie shivered. 'As if I was just a *thing*. Like Robo.'

'But we're not really *learning* anything, are we?' Angelika said. 'Why is he doing all this?'

Ethan shook his head. 'I don't know. But we *have* to find out. Right?'

'Ye-es,' Lizzie said cautiously. 'But we need to be careful. We mustn't let anyone else know what we're doing.'

'We can be a secret society!' said Tyler. 'With a badge and a password and—'

Ethan frowned at him. 'This isn't a game. The Headmaster's *dangerous*.'

'If we stand up against him, we're taking a big risk,' Lizzie said. 'And there are only four of us.'

'*Five*,' said Tyler.' The others stared at him and he

grinned. 'You've forgotten Robo. He's one of us.'

**LOOK INTO MY EYES**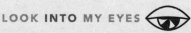

# 13

# HOMEWORK

They *had* to find out what the Headmaster was up to. Lizzie knew they were doing the right thing. But she wished they had more people to help them. What could four kids and a robot do, against an enemy like the Headmaster?

He was already inside their minds.

She felt scared and sick as she walked home with Tyler and Robo. They were taking a massive risk. If the Headmaster found out what they were doing, he only had to hypnotize them and start asking questions. They wouldn't be able to stop themselves telling him everything.

She felt even worse when they got home. Mum was asleep, and Dad wouldn't stop raving about Hazelbrook Academy.

'You two are so lucky!' he said. 'Going to that school will change your lives! If only all schools could be run like Hazelbrook.'

He'd made them some tea, brought it into the living room, and put it down on the table.

'Have this quickly,' he said. 'Then you can get on with your homework. It's really important to do it on time. Good homework is the foundation of education.'

Lizzie felt like crying. He was just spouting

something from the school website. It was like having the Headmaster peering into their home, watching them all. She drank her tea as fast as she could and went to sit down at the table.

'OK,' she said. 'Let's get on with our homework, Ty. What have you got?'

'Writing computer code.' Tyler took one of the school tablets out of his bag and turned it on. 'It all has to be ready by next Wednesday.'

Something about his voice made Lizzie look up. 'What's happening next Wednesday?

Tyler blinked. 'Did I say something about Wednesday?'

Lizzie felt as if something was crawling across the back of her neck. 'Ask me,' she said. 'Ask me about my homework.'

Tyler shrugged. 'OK. What's *your* homework?'

Before Lizzie could even think about the answer, she heard herself say, 'I'm drawing graphs, to show the frequency of metaphors and similes in Shakespeare's sonnets.'

Tyler pulled a face. 'Sounds really boring.'

Lizzie felt her mouth open again. 'Oh *no*!' she said brightly. 'Shakespeare's works are a good source of data for the paper I have to write by next Wednesday.'

Tyler looked startled. 'You said Wednesday too. But . . . that's just a coincidence. Isn't it?'

'I don't know.' Lizzie thought about it. 'Maybe we should ask someone else.'

She took out her phone and scrolled through her

contacts. Not Becky . . . or Hannah . . . or Joe . . . They wouldn't be happy if she rang them. And even Kelly didn't pick up any more when she called her.

She'd lost a lot of friends after the trouble with Blake.

Maybe Sophie? They'd stayed friends last term (well, sort of). She might just answer. Nervously Lizzie rang the number.

'Yes?' Sophie's voice said, not sounding friendly at all.

'I—um—I wanted to ask a question about the homework,' Lizzie said. 'Are you doing the—er—the Shakespeare homework?'

'The what?' Sophie sounded baffled. 'No, I haven't got anything like that.'

'Oh. So—' There was no time to think of a clever way of asking. Lizzie could tell Sophie was about to ring off. 'So what *are* you doing?'

'I'm analysing movements in the stock market,' Sophie said. 'Over the last six months.'

'Right,' Lizzie said. 'And are you—?'

'Look, I haven't got time to talk,' Sophie said impatiently. 'I know *you* don't care about school, but I do—and I have to finish this homework by next Wednesday.'

She rang off, without even bothering to say goodbye. Lizzie bit her lip. Sophie was the only one of her friends who'd stood by her last term. But now she'd changed too. *She thinks I'm a stupid vandal.*

'So?' Tyler said. 'So? Did you find out anything?'

Lizzie forced her mind back to what she was supposed to be doing. She gave Tyler a quick nod. 'Different homework, but the same day. Next Wednesday.'

They looked at each other for a moment. Then Lizzie reached for her phone again. She'd had an idea. She thought for a moment and then called Angelika.

'Hi, this is Lizzie. I was just wondering . . . what have you got for homework?'

'Homework?' Angelika sounded surprised. Then her brisk, efficient voice took over. 'I'm preparing an analysis of my cash flow and comparing it with the predictions in my original business plan at the beginning of term. When I have finished, I will have a clear picture of the viability of the coffee stall—'

'Is that for Wednesday?' Lizzie said.

'Well . . . yes.' Angelika sounded surprised. 'How did you know?'

'It looks as if *everyone's* homework has to be ready on Wednesday. So I wondered what makes Wednesday so important. And I *wondered*—' Lizzie closed her eyes for a moment, hoping she wasn't going to upset Angelika '—I wondered if there was anything special in your mother's diary for that day.'

There was a tiny pause. Then Angelika said, 'Are you asking me to *snoop on my mother*?'

'Only to *help* her,' Lizzie said. 'You think the Headmaster's hypnotized her too. And we're trying to stop him.'

Angelika hesitated. 'How would you feel if it was *your* mother?'

Lizzie thought about her mum. When she got better, maybe she would be glued to the school website, like Dad. If that happened . . . The idea made Lizzie so angry she couldn't speak for a moment. Then she said, 'If the Headmaster tried to hypnotize *her*, I'd do anything to stop him. Whatever it took.'

There was another silence. Then Angelika muttered, 'All right, I'll try. What shall I do if I find out something?'

'We need to meet,' Lizzie said. 'But not in the park. Someone might see us there. I'll think of a good place and text you. OK?'

'OK,' Angelika said. 'See you tomorrow.'

As Lizzie rang off, Tyler nudged her and held out his hands, and Lizzie looked at Tyler. 'OK. Now I just need to invent a good place for us to meet.'

Tyler held out his hands, clenched together. 'Abracadabra!' he said. 'I know a *really* good place.' He opened his fingers. In the palm of one hand was a piece of paper with some words scribbled on it. 'I used to go there a lot,' he said. 'When I was hiding from Blake.'

Lizzie uncrumpled the paper. As she read what he'd written, she started to smile. 'No one's going to see us there,' she said. 'I'll text the others and tell them.'

# 14

# PAUSE . . .

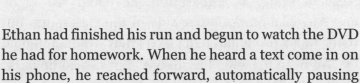

Ethan had finished his run and begun to watch the DVD he had for homework. When he heard a text come in on his phone, he reached forward, automatically pausing the video.

For a second, he felt very strange, as if he was floating up from somewhere deep underwater. *I must have been really into that film*, he thought as he picked up the phone.

It was a text from Lizzie.

**Meet tomorrow morning break** it said.

**Where?** he texted back.

**In drama studio under stage**

He didn't understand that. **How under?**

**Trapdoor OK?**

**OK**

He was longing to call and find out why Lizzie wanted them to meet. But he had no idea who might be listening at her end. It was better to be patient and wait till tomorrow. Putting his phone down, he reached out to start the video again. There was only half an hour gone. He had to watch another *sixty-five* minutes. And it was all pointless. He'd already forgotten the first thirty . . .

Before he could finish the thought, the video dragged

him back in. For an instant, he was aware of tiny figures racing across the screen. Then his mind went blank and he didn't remember anything after that.

Next morning, at registration, he could see Lizzie and Angelika on the other side of the classroom. But there was a drone hovering over their heads. It would be stupid to try and talk—maybe even dangerous. He would just have to be patient for a bit longer.

At least that ought to be easy He was going straight off to football after registration, so he wouldn't know much about the next two hours. That was what he thought, anyway.

But it didn't work out quite the way he expected . . .

The game began like the others. He changed into his football kit and jogged out on to the field, feeling his mind go blank as his boots touched the grass. *Here we go. Another two hours stolen out of my life* . . .

But then something different happened.

When his mind woke up again, he wasn't jogging back into the changing room with all the others. He was standing stock still in the middle of the football pitch with twenty-one boys milling around him, looking confused.

The reserves were standing on the touchline, whispering to each other. And Mr Wasu was *yelling*.

'Ethan! What are you doing, boy? You just *stopped*—

right in the middle of a kick. What were you *thinking*?'

'I—' Ethan blinked and looked around. He had no idea what Mr Wasu was talking about. But he knew what would happen if he tried to explain. So he muttered, 'Sorry. Just lost it for a moment.'

'Lost it?' Mr Wasu rolled his eyes and clutched at his head. 'You're our star player and you just—*lost it*?' His mouth opened and shut as he struggled for words. At last, he shrugged and waved his hand. 'Never mind,' he said wearily. 'Play on.'

For a split second, Ethan didn't know what to do. *How do I start from here?* Then his legs took over and he didn't think any more.

Afterwards, at break, it was hard to get away from the changing room. All the other boys came crowding round him, asking questions.

'What happened out there, Shorty?'

'Mr Wasu said you just stopped.'

'If we'd been playing another school, they'd have *murdered* us.'

'What were you *doing*?'

There was no way of answering the questions. And Ethan was desperate to get away. 'I just—um—couldn't move for a moment,' he said. 'Had cramp—er—in my back.'

'In your *back*?'

Ethan had no idea where footballers got cramp, but he'd obviously said something peculiar. They fired off lots more questions about where it hurt and how bad it was. He knew they were being friendly, but he wished they'd stop. He had to get to the drama studio.

As soon as he'd changed, he headed for the door, grinning over his shoulder as they all shouted advice.

'And you ought to drink more water,' Piotr said. 'That's good for cramp.'

Ethan nodded energetically. 'Great idea. I'll go and get a drink now. See you!' And he was out of there, heading for the drama studio as fast as he could go without running. But he wasn't concentrating. He couldn't stop thinking about what had happened out on the football field. *Why had he stopped? And why had that made everyone else stop too?*

Because he was in a hurry, he forgot to check for drones until he was halfway down the drama studio corridor. Then he suddenly remembered. And when he glanced over his shoulder, there *was* a drone, just coming round the corner behind him.

What an idiot he was! That corridor didn't go anywhere else. If someone was monitoring that drone, they would already know where he was going. Would it be safer to turn back?

Surely no one could watch *all* the drones. Not *all* the time. He was only taking a tiny risk. Diving into the drama studio, he shut the door behind him, very quickly, so the drone couldn't follow. Then he watched it, through the glass panel in the top of the door. It hovered around for a moment and then floated back up the corridor.

When it was out of sight, he went across the studio and jumped up onto the stage. The curtains were pulled shut. He ducked between them and found Robo, standing at the side of the stage. Good. Tyler was still there, then. And that probably meant the others were too.

'Hello?' he called softly. 'Sorry I'm late.'

There was a little pause. Then the trapdoor lifted and Tyler's head poked out, looking very dusty. 'You *scared* us,' he said. 'We didn't know who it was.'

'Sorry,' Ethan said as he lowered himself through the hole. 'I came as fast as I could. Why are we meeting?'

'It's about Wednesday,' said Lizzie. 'It seems as if everyone's homework has to be ready by Wednesday. So I asked Angelika to look in her mum's diary, to see if anything special was happening then.'

Ethan looked at Angelika. 'And?'

'I did look,' Angelika muttered. 'And there *is* something. But I don't know what it means. And I couldn't look any more. Mum nearly caught me doing it.'

'What was it?' Ethan said.

'On Wednesday, it says *PMV Rehearsal.*'

PMV? Ethan frowned. Where had he seen those letters before?

But Angelika hadn't finished. 'And on Thursday it has *PMV Security Check.* At five o'clock in the morning. And then it's in again at ten o'clock, but that time it just says *PMV.*'

'We've been trying to work out what it stands for,' Tyler said. 'But we can't think of anything.'

Ethan couldn't think of anything either. Except that he *knew* he'd seen those letters before. PMV. Where was it? What did they mean? 'Hang on a minute,' he muttered.

He shut his eyes and tried to picture them. Three black letters. PMV. They'd been in a list somewhere, with other letters above and below them. And he'd seen the list . . . on his computer screen. Yes, that was right. But he hadn't taken notice of the PMV thing, because he'd been . . . he'd been . . .

*He'd been concentrating on the Drone Management folder.*

'Got it!' he said, opening his eyes. 'I think I know where we can find out some more. Just wait while I log on.'

He held his breath as he took out his phone and put in Mrs Maron's ID and her password. Maybe he was wrong. Or maybe the folder had been deleted. But, no, when he got into the network it was there, just as he'd remembered it. He opened it and read down the list of documents. There were lots of letters and emails.

'Well?' Lizzie said impatiently.

'Wait a moment while I look.' He had to read three of the letters and two emails before he took in what they meant. When he understood, he couldn't speak for a moment.

'Is it important?' Angelika said.

'I-I think so.' Ethan read the last email again, to be absolutely sure. Then he swallowed and looked up. 'PMV means *Prime Minister's Visit*.'

Angelika's eyes opened wide. 'You mean—the Prime Minister's coming *here*?'

Ethan nodded. 'On Thursday.'

 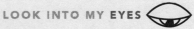

# 15

# CAUGHT

'I don't understand,' Tyler said. 'Why would the Prime Minister come to Hazelbrook?'

Ethan looked back at the longest letter. 'To see what a fantastic school it is. That's why we're rehearsing on Wednesday. We're going to put on a brilliant show for the Prime Minister on Thursday—to prove Hazelbrook's turned us all into stars.'

'There must be hundreds of schools wanting a visit like that,' Lizzie said. 'How did the Headmaster get the Prime Minister to come *here*?'

Ethan pulled a face. 'There was a video conference. **Right?** Once people actually see the Headmaster— once he gets them to look into his eyes—he always gets his own way, doesn't he?'

'Why are you so worried?' Tyler said. 'It's only a *visit.*'

'It's not just about this school,' Ethan said bitterly. 'It's about convincing the Prime Minister that *all* schools should be like Hazelbrook. If the visit goes well, the Headmaster will be taking over hundreds of other schools. Maybe every school in the country.'

'And what's going to impress the Prime Minister?' Lizzie said. 'It's Tyler's amazing robot. And your brilliant football skills.'

'And my business plan,' Angelika said. 'And the thing Lizzie's writing about Shakespeare's grammar—'

'And all the other kids doing super-wonderful things they couldn't do before the Headmaster came to Hazelbrook.' Lizzie was so angry she could hardly speak. 'He's getting *us* to help him trick the Prime Minister.'

Tyler frowned. 'But it's all fake. We can't really do those things.'

'The Prime Minister won't know that.' Angelika said miserably. 'Hazelbrook's going to look like the perfect school. The way all other schools should be.'

'The way they *will* be,' said Lizzie. 'If the Headmaster takes them over.'

'That mustn't happen!' Ethan thumped his fists together. 'We mustn't *let* it happen.'

Tyler jumped up. 'Let's ruin the show! Let's turn it into a disaster!'

'If only we could,' said Angelika. 'But we won't even know what we're doing, will we? We'll just be following the Headmaster's instructions.'

'But there's going to be a rehearsal, isn't there?' Lizzie said slowly. 'When we've had that, maybe we can work out what the Headmaster's making us do. That ought to give us time to work out how to ruin it. If we each wreck our own part of the show—'

'—that's FOUR disasters.' Suddenly, Ethan looked excited. 'With lots of reporters and photographers around to see!'

Angelika clapped her hands. 'Publicity is Power— that's in my business plan. If Hazelbrook gets lots of *bad* publicity, the Headmaster won't be able to take over any more schools.'

'We can do it!' Lizzie said. 'I know we can do it!'

'But it has to be secret.' Ethan looked round at them all. 'Right?'

'Right.' The others all said it together.

Ethan grinned and tapped at his phone, and Robo's voice sounded above their heads.

**'RIGHT.'**

They were all grinning as they hauled themselves up through the trapdoor and brushed the dust off their clothes. Lizzie helped Tyler lift Robo down from the stage and then she ran across to open the door.

All the welcomers were standing outside, blocking the corridor in both directions.

Lizzie stood in the doorway, with her mouth open, as Blake stepped forward. He put his foot out, to stop her closing the door.

'The Headmaster wants to see you all,' he said. 'In his office. Now.'

*It's my fault!* Lizzie thought miserably, as the welcomers marched them down the corridor. *I've got Tyler into trouble. I ought to have known it was too dangerous. We should never have got involved. I should have—*

Should have what? Let the Headmaster carry on with his plans? Ignore the lies that he made her speak?

That would have been even worse. No, Ethan was right. They had to stop the Headmaster.

When they reached the office, Blake lifted his hand to knock on the door. But, before he could touch it, the Headmaster's voice spoke from inside.

'Come in. All of you.'

Blake opened the door and stood back to let the other welcomers push everyone else inside. He gave Lizzie a quick look as she passed him, as if there was something he wanted to say. But he didn't speak. Just waited until they were all in the office and then came in after them and closed the door.

The Headmaster was standing on the far side of the room. It was impossible to tell where he was looking, because of his dark glasses, but Lizzie felt as if he was staring straight at her. It seemed as though his eyes were drilling into her. Reading her mind. She was so frightened she couldn't stop trembling.

And he wasn't a hologram this time. He was really there. With them. In the room.

She made herself lift her head and look back at him, but that was even worse, because she couldn't see his eyes. It was like staring into a deep, dark pit, knowing that somewhere, in the darkness, an enemy was watching her.

When he spoke at last, his voice was clear and cold. 'You were meeting in secret,' he said. 'One of you was filmed entering the drama studio—where you had no reason to be.'

'We only just got there in time,' Blake said. 'If we hadn't hurried—'

'Silence.' The Headmaster didn't raise his voice, but

 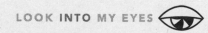

Blake's mouth snapped shut.

*He's scared too*, Lizzie thought.

Light flickered on the dark lenses as the Headmaster turned his head, looking from one face to another. His pale mouth twisted into a thin, unpleasant smile. 'No doubt you thought that your meeting was secret. But, naturally, the drama studio is fitted with microphones.' He stepped over to his desk and clicked the computer mouse.

Suddenly, the room was full of whispering voices. Even though they were muffled, most of the words were clear.

' . . . the Headmaster will be taking over hundreds of other schools . . .'

' . . . what's going to impress the Prime Minister? . . . He's getting *us* to help him . . .'

'We mustn't *let* it happen . . .'

And then Tyler's voice, sounding loud and excited. 'Let's ruin the show! Let's turn it into a disaster!'

The Headmaster let the recording run right to the end before he switched it off. Then he looked up at them all. 'I assume you are expecting some kind of punishment.'

Tyler's hand slid into Lizzie's. She could feel it shaking and she squeezed his fingers hard.

'You underestimate me.' For a moment, the Headmaster sounded almost amused. 'My plans cannot be upset by *children*. The Prime Minister will visit on Thursday, as planned. By the end of that visit, it will be clear to everyone that all schools should be like

Hazelbrook.'

'No!' Lizzie said.

The Headmaster ignored her. 'In a few months, the Hazelbrook method will be rolled out across the whole country. I shall be in charge of the entire education system—making sure it produces the right kind of workers, in the right numbers.'

'Like a factory farm!' Lizzie said. 'That's *evil*.'

'It will be efficient,' the Headmaster said coldly.

'No!' Tyler shouted. 'You won't get away with it! We'll stop you—somehow!'

For an extraordinary moment, it actually looked as though the Headmaster might laugh. 'On the contrary,' he said. 'You four will play starring roles on Thursday. You will convince the Prime Minister to hand over everything to me.'

'No!' Ethan said. 'We won't do it!'

'You will not be able to stop yourselves,' the Headmaster said scornfully. Suddenly, his hands moved, taking off his glasses before any of them could look away.

*No!* Lizzie thought. *I mustn't—*

But it was too late. She was already staring into the Headmaster's eyes. Being pulled in and down, deeper and deeper—

YOU ARE GOING TO PLAY A KEY PART IN MY PLANS

This time, it felt as if the words were being spoken right inside her brain. Whispered by her own mind. She screwed up her fists, concentrating on trying to keep them out, on keeping hold of her own thoughts. But the voice in her brain wouldn't stop . . .

YOU WILL NOT BE ABLE TO STOP YOURSELF. BECAUSE IF YOU TRY—

And then—KKKRRRZZZ!!! A sharp, fierce pain shot through her head, as if someone was knocking red hot nails into it. All the breath was knocked out of her body, and as she doubled up, she heard Tyler scream and she knew he was feeling it too.

*Stop! Stop!!* yelled her mind. *Anything to stop the pain!*

The next thing she knew, she was standing in the information hub, staring at Mr Bains. And he was staring back at her, with a slightly puzzled look on his face.

'Are you sure you want *those* books?' he said.

'Yes, please.' Lizzie had no idea what she'd asked for. The words came out of her mouth automatically.

Mr Bains smiled—a slightly disappointed smile— and pointed across the room. 'You'd better go over there. I'll bring them to you.'

She sat down and a few minutes later he came across with a pile of books in his arms.

'Here you are,' he said. 'I'm afraid you'll find them rather—dry.'

'Reading has nothing to do with pleasure,' Lizzie heard herself say.

Mr Bains stared for a moment, as if the words were

hanging in the air between them. Then he put the books down on the table and went back to his desk.

Lizzie looked at the pile in front of her.

*Shakespeare's Use of the Subjunctive*

*Medieval Survivals in Shakespearean Grammar*

*The Influence of Latin on Shakespeare's Prose Style*

She didn't even know what the titles meant. Opening one of the books, she found herself staring at long words and complicated tables. The Headmaster must have told her to ask for that book—but why? What was the point of making her read something she couldn't understand?

*No. I won't.* She started pushing the book away, but as she closed it—*KKKRRRZZZ!!!* The pain hit her again, even worse than before. She snatched the book back and wrenched it open, just to stop the terrible burning in her head.

When the pain started fading, she looked down and began to read the incomprehensible words.

# 16

# FIVE GOALS

When Ethan came back to himself, he was sitting in the PE classroom with the other footballers. He couldn't remember how he'd got out of the Headmaster's office. He couldn't remember anything about what had happened there—except the words that seemed to be burnt into his brain.

YOU ARE GOING TO PLAY A KEY PART IN MY PLANS

YOU WILL NOT BE ABLE TO STOP YOURSELF . . .

Those words—and the memory of terrible, unbearable pain.

Mr Wasu smiled and turned on the whiteboard. 'I have some new instructions,' he said. 'From now on, we'll all be watching the training videos together. But you mustn't stop watching football at home. It's a great way to improve your skills. I hope you all see lots of games on television?'

The only football matches Ethan had ever seen were the videos he watched for homework and he couldn't remember anything about those. But everyone else in the room was shouting enthusiastically.

'Yeah! I always watch the big games.'

'Everyone in our house does!'

'Best things on TV!'

'Well, you'll never see anything better than *this*,' Mr Wasu said, waving a DVD at them. 'I'm going to show you one of the greatest games of football that's ever been played. Barcelona v Bayer Leverkusen in 2012.'

And the big kids *knew* about it. Ethan was amazed. They started waving their arms and yelling things like 'Messi!' and 'Brilliant!' and 'Five goals!' as if they'd seen the match yesterday. And they were so keen to watch it that they shut up and sat still the moment Mr Wasu started the video.

*What happens if I shut my eyes*? Ethan wondered suddenly. *Suppose I just don't watch?* Leaning forward, so no one would notice, he starting shutting his eyes and—

KKKRRRZZZ!!!

The pain was so sudden and so fierce that he gasped, before he could stop himself. Mr Wasu stopped the video and turned round, looking concerned.

'Ethan? Are you all right?'

'It's—' Ethan wanted to explain, more than ever before. But he could guess what would happen if he tried. 'It's just cramp,' he said, when he could speak.

'Again?' Mr Wasu frowned. 'Maybe you should see a doctor.'

'It's OK,' Ethan said. 'Honestly.' Now the pain was gone he felt weak and shaky, but it was no use saying that. 'Please—'

*Please go on with the video*, he was going to say. But before he could say the words, he looked up at the screen—and there were the players, frozen in mid-run.

Piotr saw him looking and he laughed. 'Imagine if they could see themselves,' he said. 'If they suddenly woke up and found they'd just stopped.'

'Like Ethan this morning,' said Onil.

Everyone fell about laughing—except Ethan. He was staring at the screen with his eyes wide open, remembering the last time he'd watched a football video. Yesterday evening, for homework. And when the text had come in, he'd paused the video.

And then *he'd* paused, in the middle of the next practice match.

Was that just a coincidence? Or were the videos actually connected with the games they played?

It seemed like a crazy idea. But maybe he could remember this video, and then remember what he did on the football field. And if he could *remember* . . .

'Let's go on,' he said to Mr Wasu. 'I'm fine now.'

Mr Wasu nodded and reached for the remote control. Screwing up his fists, Ethan stared at the screen, thinking, *This time I WILL remember. Remember, remember, REMEMBER . . .*

But it was no use. As soon as the figures on the screen started moving, his brain misted over and all his thoughts dis . . . app . . . eared . . .

When he came round, all the other boys were blinking and looking around. Just like him. But they were talking as if they remembered every minute of the video.

'Yay! Brilliant game!'

'Best I've ever seen!'

'Classic!'

Piotr nudged Ethan. 'Enjoy it?'

For a second, there was a hazy picture in Ethan's mind. Men in football kit . . . the ball slamming into the goal . . . over and over again . . . 'Messi's amazing,' he heard himself say. '*Five goals!*'

So maybe he *did* he remember—with some part of his brain. But there was no time to wonder about that. Mr Wasu was hustling them all down to the changing room.

'Get your kit on—fast,' he said. 'Get out there while you're still feeling inspired. Start *playing.*'

As he laced up his boots, Ethan tried to work out what was going on. Lots of people watched football videos, to see what the great players did. But that didn't suddenly turn *them* into brilliant footballers. He had to be missing something.

'Hurry up, boy!' Mr Wasu yelled across the changing room. 'Stop dreaming and *get out there!*'

The others were jogging out on to the pitch as Ethan tied up his second boot. *If only I could see myself playing*, he thought. *If only—*

But he could! The changing room had small high windows—looking out over the football pitch. All he had to do was set his phone to video and prop it up on the window ledge. It was risky, but it just might work.

He climbed onto one of the benches and leaned the phone against the window. It wasn't going to take a great film, but it would tell him what he needed to know. He started the camera, jumped down, and ran out on to the pitch just as Mr Wasu started bellowing his name.

When he came round at the end of the game, he was so tired he could hardly speak. But he couldn't wait to catch his breath. He had to move his phone before anyone noticed it. The other boys were shouting something at him, but he didn't listen. He raced into the changing room, jumped onto the bench, grabbed the phone, shoved it into the pocket of his shorts, jumped down and—

And then he was swamped. Twenty-one tall, hefty boys piled through the door and flung themselves at him, ruffling his hair and slapping him on the back. They were singing at the tops of their voices, like a football crowd.

'*Five goals, fi-ive goals, five goals, five goals*
*Five goals, fi-ive goals, fi-ve GOALS!'*

And the two reserves were just as excited. 'Yo, Ethan!' Oscar high-fived him with a massive grin on his face.

'Who needs Messi?' Noah shouted. 'We've got Ethan—the pocket tornado!'

Ethan was completely swamped. He couldn't have spoken even if he'd wanted to—and he knew the pain would get him if he tried. He just grinned and punched the air triumphantly.

But it wasn't because he'd scored five goals . . .

Mr Wasu was grinning too. 'I was right,' he said. 'That video really inspired you all.'

When Ethan finally had a chance to look at his phone, the battery was flat. How much of the match had it filmed before it died? He was desperate to find out, but he hadn't got his charger at school.

When the bell rang for lunch, he was feeling frustrated and impatient. But, as he walked into the canteen, the first thing he noticed was the long, long queue at the drinks stall. And the big banner draped above it:

NEW THIS WEEK!
GINGER HOT CHOCOLATE!!
WITH WHIPPED CREAM AND HONEYCOMB
CRUMBS!!!

He didn't care about the hot chocolate—but it made him think of something else about Angelika. Her phone was the same as his. Maybe he could borrow her charger.

He couldn't just go across and ask, though. There was a drone hovering right by her stall and another one on the other side of the canteen. It would be safer to join the end of the queue, as if he just wanted to buy a drink.

When he reached the front, he ordered ginger hot chocolate. It sounded disgusting, but he knew the electric whisk would make enough noise to cover his voice. When Angelika started whipping the cream, he spoke very softly, standing with his back to the drone, so only Angelika could see his lips moving.

'Can I borrow your phone charger? There's something I need to look at.'

'It's at home.' Angelika put the mug of hot chocolate onto the counter. Very quickly, she piped whipped cream on top of it—forming a word no one else could see. *COME*.

Ethan frowned. But Angelika hadn't finished. She smoothed the cream and reached for the pot of honeycomb crumbs, sprinkling them on to form words. *4 PM*.

*Yes,* Ethan thought. *Yes—we need to talk about what's happened. To see if there's still anything we can do.* He grinned at Angelika. 'Perfect!' he said—as if he was talking about the hot chocolate.

'Here,' Angelika handed him a plastic spoon. 'You need this for the cream.'

Ethan scraped the spoon across the mug, breaking up her message and scratching some letters of his own. *TELL L + T.* Then he lifted the mug to his lips and took a long swig.

It was even more disgusting than he'd expected.

# 17
# WE CAN DO IT!

Lizzie and Tyler were standing in the lunch queue on the other side of the canteen, with Robo wedged in between them—because Tyler refused to leave him outside. Tyler was looking wistfully across at Angelika's new banner and Lizzie wished she could buy him a mug of hot chocolate. But they hadn't got enough money. Not even for one mug, to share.

'Bad for your teeth,' she whispered.

'I know,' Tyler said sadly. 'I don't *really* want any. I was just trying to imagine what it tastes like.'

*Much too sweet*, Lizzie was going to say. But before she could speak, Angelika suddenly yelled across the canteen.

'Hey, Tyler, I need help. Can your robot whip cream?'

Tyler looked at Lizzie. 'Do you think he can?'

'Must be able to.' Lizzie gave Tyler a little push. 'Look—Ethan's over there. He'll help you.'

Tyler steered Robo across the canteen and Angelika leaned over the counter, holding out the cream whisk. *Don't say anything stupid*, Lizzie thought. She could see two drones hovering very close to them. *Remember the Headmaster's watching.*

Ethan muttered something and Tyler took the

cream whisk and clipped it into one of Robo's hands. *I hope they've got it right*, Lizzie thought, *or everyone's going to get covered in cream*. She started working her way over there, so she would be close if anything went wrong.

But it didn't. Robo lowered the whisk into the cream and everyone in the queue started clapping.

'Hot chocolate with added robot power!' someone shouted.

Mrs Maron was just walking into the canteen and Angelika called across to her. 'Look at this! Tyler's robot really *can* help on my stall! You said we ought to hold a proper business meeting. Can we have it tonight?'

Mrs Maron looked as if she was going to say no. But Angelika didn't give her a chance to speak. She went on talking, waving her hands about eagerly.

'Just think how great it will look, having Robo serve my hot chocolate! He could do it on special occasions! When we have important visitors!'

Mrs Maron hesitated. *Is she thinking about Thursday?* Lizzie wondered. *And impressing the Prime Minister?*

Angelika was still chattering away. 'We need to work out the details, to make sure it works smoothly. How about if Tyler and Lizzie come home with us, after school?'

'And Robo,' Tyler said. 'He has to come too.'

Mrs Maron looked down at his eager face and he gave her a wide, innocent smile. All right,' she said slowly. 'I'll phone your parents and tell them.'

She swept off, her high heels clicking on the hard floor, and Angelika grinned at Lizzie and Tyler. 'Result!' she said. 'You two should have a free hot chocolate. Get working on it, Robo.'

Seconds later, they were both holding mugs heaped high with whipped cream and honeycomb toffee crumbs. When Tyler took a sip, he got cream all over the end of his nose.

When they walked into Angelika's bedroom after school, Lizzie really felt she was going to a business meeting. The room was exactly like an office, with a desk under the window, a filing cabinet and a tall metal cupboard. (Was that where Angelika kept her clothes?) The bed was pushed right over to one side, and covered with cushions, to make it look like a sofa.

Tyler stared round it. 'I—er—cool room,' he muttered.

'I need to work at home,' Angelika said, in a brisk, mechanical voice. 'You don't succeed in business without working long hours.'

She was standing at the desk, staring through the window. Suddenly, she gave a little wave and ran out into the hall. Lizzie went to the window to see who she'd waved at.

'It's Ethan,' she whispered.

A few seconds later, they heard the front door open and close, very quietly. Angelika crept back into the room with Ethan close behind her.

'Mum's in the kitchen,' she muttered. 'It's best if she doesn't know Ethan's here. If she sees him, she'll guess we're not really talking about hot chocolate.'

Ethan frowned. 'And she'd tell the Headmaster?'

'It's not her fault,' Angelika said miserably. 'It's *him*. He's made her like that.'

'He's made everyone like that,' said Lizzie. 'A whole school full of people, all doing what he says. Like an army.'

'But why don't they realize?' Tyler said. 'Why is it only us?'

Ethan shrugged. 'Maybe he's made other people good at things they actually *like*. If I loved football, I'd probably be too happy to wonder *how* I'd suddenly turned into a star.'

'Well, how *did* you?' Lizzie said. 'How could the Headmaster *tell* you to be good at football? It's not like me spouting stuff out of books, or Tyler making a robot. You're playing with twenty-one other people—and every game's different.'

Ethan grinned and waved his phone at her. 'I think I've just solved that. Angelika, is it OK if I play this on your computer?'

'Help yourself.' Angelika tossed him the lead.

Ethan plugged in his phone and found the film he'd taken that morning. 'Watch this.'

For a couple of seconds, the others looked puzzled. Then Tyler gave a yelp. 'There's Ethan! Hey, Ethan, you're going really fast.'

'And that's a great pass!' Angelika clapped her

hands. 'Look—you beat *Ben Crawshaw*!'

'Shh,' Ethan said. 'Just keep watching. And try to remember what you see, especially the goals.'

They had to wait a while for the first goal, but when it came it was sensational. Ethan raced down the pitch, with two of the other team chasing after him, and he floated the ball over the goalkeeper's head—from yards up the pitch—sending it straight into the net.

Fifteen minutes later, he did it again, sending the ball low and straight past the goalie's right side and into the net. As if it was the easiest thing in the world.

Then it was over. The video stopped and Ethan unplugged his phone. 'Wait,' he said, tapping at the computer. 'I haven't finished yet. Now watch . . . this.'

This time it was a YouTube video. He muted the sound and, when he set it going, they saw two teams in the middle of a game. One team in blue and red stripes and the other in white. One of the men in blue and red raced down the pitch, with two white players after him. He floated the ball over the goalkeeper's head and into the net—from yards up the pitch.

Angelika gasped. 'That's exactly like—'

Ethan held up his hand to stop her. 'Just keep watching.'

The video cut to the next goal. The same blue and red player was running down the pitch, closer to the goal this time. He shot the ball straight past the goalie—from exactly the position where Ethan had been when he scored *his* second goal.

Ethan stopped the video. 'That was Lionel Messi,'

he said. 'He scored three more goals in that match—and I scored three more in ours. If I'd been able to video those, I bet they would have looked *exactly the same* as his.'

Tyler gasped. 'You mean the Headmaster's made you play like *Lionel Messi*?'

'It's not just me,' Ethan said. 'We were all acting out that match—because we'd just been watching it. We don't really play at all. It's like a ballet, where the dancers learn all the moves in advance. But we don't realize, because we can't—we can't—'

He'd forgotten the pain. It sliced into him and he doubled up, putting his hands over his mouth to stop himself screeching. For a moment, he thought he was going to be sick.

'We get it, we get it,' Lizzie said quickly. 'You don't need to say any more.'

'Sit down over here.' Angelika steered him across to the bed. 'Shall I get you some water?'

Ethan shook his head. 'So you know what just happened?' he muttered, when he could speak.

'Oh, I know all right,' Lizzie said fiercely. 'And I bet the others do as well. That's what the Headmaster's done to us, to make sure we don't spoil his plans.'

'Can't we spoil them without talking?' said Tyler. 'Maybe Ethan could break a leg.'

'No chance.' Angelika shook her head. 'Remember what the Headmaster said? *You are going to play a key part in my plans. You will not be able to stop yourself.*'

'Well, maybe *I* could break his leg,' Tyler said.

Ethan's face changed suddenly, as if he'd put on a mask. He jumped up and glared at Tyler. 'Don't you dare come near me! If you try to wreck the football, I'll—I'll *smash Robo*!'

'No!' wailed Tyler.

'Shh! Shh!' Angelika waved her hands desperately. 'If you start shouting, Mum will hear.'

'Stop it, both of you!' Lizzie said. 'Can't you see what's happening? The Headmaster's done this.'

Angelika grabbed Ethan's fists, pulling them away from Tyler. 'You don't *care* about the football, Ethan. You know you don't. The Headmaster's *hypnotized* you into behaving as if you do. So you go crazy just thinking about your star turn being wrecked.'

'That's right!' Lizzie put her arm round Tyler. 'Quick! Think about something else.'

Tyler was still half sobbing, but Ethan got what she meant. 'Yes,' he said. '*Yes!* You're a genius, Lizzie! Tyler, think about something else, like—um—like wrecking Angelika's coffee stall. How does that make you feel?'

Tyler looked startled for a second. Then he began to smile. 'I can see a great way to do that,' he said.

Angelika darted forward, as if she was going to smack him, but Ethan pulled Tyler out of the way.

'It's OK,' he said. 'I was just testing. Don't you see? *That's the answer!*'

Lizzie thought about it. 'You mean . . . we can't stop *ourselves* doing what the Headmaster's ordered. But Angelika could stop you. And I could stop Tyler. And—'

'That's right!' Ethan nodded. 'We can still do it!'

'But that doesn't work,' Angelika said. 'If you *know* I'm trying to stop you—'

'You don't *have* to know!' Ethan said, looking round. 'Have you got some paper?'

Angelika handed him a sheet and he tore it neatly into four pieces. He wrote one of their names on each piece, then folded them up and shook them together in his hands.

'OK,' he said. 'Take a name and read it—without showing the rest of us.'

'But suppose we get our own names?' Tyler said.

'Then we put the papers back and try again. Come on.'

The first time, Lizzie and Angelika both pulled out their own names. The second time, Tyler pulled out his. But the third time, it worked perfectly. They all looked down at their pieces of paper, nodded, and pushed them into their pockets.

'Good,' said Ethan. 'Now we mustn't talk any more, in case we give anything away. We have to stay apart— and trust each other to get things right. Yes?'

'Yes!' The others all said it together.

'Right, then, I'm off.' Ethan grinned. 'Sorry for interrupting your important business meeting.'

And he slipped out of the house so quietly they didn't even hear him close the front door.

---

*It's a good plan,* Lizzie thought, as she and Tyler went home in the back of Mrs Maron's car. *Only—what about my bit of it?*

The piece of paper in her pocket had Ethan's name on it. How on earth was she going to wreck a football match? Cover the pitch with jam? That would take about ten thousand jars. Give all the players sleeping pills? That was much too dangerous—and where would she get the pills?

What could she possibly do?

# 18

# BREAKING NEWS

Ethan was thinking about his part of the plan as he cycled home. He'd landed up with the piece of paper that said TYLER—just what he wanted. Because Tyler's star turn was bound to involve his precious robot. And there was something brilliant Robo could do to wreck the Headmaster's schemes. Totally, utterly brilliant . . .

Ethan smiled as he pedalled along the road, working out how he was going to make it happen.

'You're late! Where have you been?'

He hadn't even reached the front door when Auntie Beryl opened it. For the first few seconds, he couldn't do anything except gape at her.

'I trusted you,' she said. 'I trusted you to come home and start on your homework. But I get back early and what do I find? You're not there! Where have you been?'

He couldn't tell her the truth. If he did, she might get on the phone to Mrs Maron. And if Mrs Maron knew where he'd been, she might get suspicious and tell the Headmaster. Ethan could just imagine what would happen next. Could almost hear the Headmaster's cold, whispering voice: *What did you do when you met at Angelika Maron's house? You will tell me everything . . .*

And he would tell. He wouldn't be able to stop himself.

'Well?' Auntie Beryl was still standing in the doorway, tapping her foot. 'I'm waiting.'

'I've been cycling,' Ethan said quickly. 'It's good extra training.'

Auntie Beryl looked at him suspiciously. 'What about your running?'

'I'll do that next—as soon as I've put my bike away. The cycling was extra. Because I need to be super-fit.'

'For Thursday?' Auntie Beryl said.

'I—what?' Ethan looked at her.

'*That's* what I was waiting to tell you.' Suddenly, she was smiling. 'I've just seen it on the website. The Prime Minister's visiting your school on Thursday!'

So that was why she'd been so annoyed he was late! She couldn't wait to share the news. Just in time, Ethan remembered to look surprised.

'Isn't it exciting!' Auntie Beryl said. 'Will you be doing anything special for the Prime Minister?'

'I might . . . be playing football.'

Auntie Beryl beamed. 'Well, you must have three lamb chops for tea. You need building up.'

Wednesday started with assembly, for the whole school. When Ethan walked into the hall, with the rest of his tutor group, Mrs Maron was already up on the stage, standing at the lectern, flicking through a pile of papers.

When everyone was sitting down, she looked up and cleared her throat. 'As you know,' she said, 'today is rehearsal day. We're going to spend the whole day going through the programme for the Prime Minister's visit, to make sure it runs smoothly tomorrow. We want Hazelbrook to shine like a splendid sun.'

Ethan stared up at her, wondering if she knew what she was saying. Or was *her* mind blank?

'Please listen carefully,' she said. 'I shall read through the programme once only. When I have finished, you will all go to your allotted places. For today's rehearsal, the Headmaster will be standing in for the Prime Minister. He will arrive at the front entrance of the school in ten minutes and we shall perform the entire programme, exactly as it will be carried out on Thursday.'

The other teachers looked at each other nervously. Ethan wasn't surprised. They were only going to hear the programme read once. And there was only going to be one practice. He could almost hear the teachers thinking, *It will never work.*

But it would, of course. The whole thing would run like clockwork.

As if they were all wind-up toys.

Mrs Maron cleared her throat and began to read. 'The Prime Minister will be met by all twenty of our welcomers, dressed in their best school uniform. Tyler Warren will also be present. He and his robot will accompany the Prime Minister throughout the day.'

*Yes!*

That was the moment Ethan had been waiting for.

He needed to know what Robo was doing, to work out a way of using him to wreck the visit. And this was even better than he'd hoped. Robo was going to be with the Prime Minister *all the time*. Whatever happened, he would be there.

Watching.

'The robot will a deliver a short, recorded speech of welcome,' Mrs Maron said, 'and give the Prime Minister a decorated copy of the day's programme, designed and produced by our sixth-form artists. Then the Prime Minister will go on . . .'

Yes, yes, and YES! Ethan's brain was whirring, working out the details of his plan. He was so excited that he almost missed his own name as Mrs Maron read out instructions for the two football teams.

# 19

# REHEARSAL

Lizzie was listening much more carefully than Ethan. Somewhere in what Mrs Maron was saying, she had to find a chance to ruin the football match.

'Footballers, you will start the day by watching a video,' Mrs Maron was saying. 'The Prime Minister will have a short coffee break at eleven—' she lifted her head and smiled at Angelika '—before coming out to watch you play football at half past eleven. You will practise all that this morning. Then you will spend the afternoon washing your kit and cleaning your boots, ready for tomorrow.'

Lizzie chewed her lip. That DVD was important. But how could she use it to wreck the match? She was so busy thinking about it that she missed most of what Mrs Maron was saying—until she heard her own name.

'Our next superstar will be Lizzie Warren.' Mrs Maron looked up at her, to make sure she was listening.' Lizzie will be in the information hub, finishing the paper she is writing on Shakespeare's use of grammar. The Prime Minister will have a chance to question her about it after lunch.'

*Oh, great,* Lizzie thought. *And I bet I'll have all the right answers.*

Mrs Maron turned over to the last page of her notes.

'Finally,' she said, 'the Prime Minister's party will come to the main hall, where the whole school will already be assembled. Blake Vinney will deliver a farewell speech in Russian, Mandarin, and Arabic—'

Blake? Speaking Mandarin? Lizzie couldn't wait to hear that.

Mrs Maron hadn't quite finished. 'Blake will be wearing special clothes designed and made by the sixth-form textiles class.'

There was a loud splutter on Lizzie's right. She glanced round quickly and saw Blake with his mouth open. It looked as though he hadn't known about the special clothes. She had to struggle to stop herself grinning. They were bound to be . . . unusual. And Blake hated looking stupid.

His horrified expression only lasted for a second. Then he was smiling, as if he'd been given a special honour. But Lizzie knew what she'd seen. She hoped the textiles class had made something really ridiculous for him to wear. Like a tutu.

For one glorious moment, she imagined Blake as a ballet dancer, trying to pirouette across the stage. He wouldn't be able to do it, of course, however hard he tried. Ballet dancers had to practise for years. No one could just stand up and *do* it, however fit they were.

No one . . .

That was *it*! An amazing idea shot into her head, like a burst of dazzling sunlight. *She knew how to wreck the football match tomorrow!* She forgot all about Blake and his special clothes and started trying to work out what she was going to do. It wouldn't be easy, but she had to find a way.

It was such a *fantastic* idea!

She had to fight to stop herself grinning as Mrs Maron dismissed them all.

Lizzie went straight to the information hub. Mr Bains had given her a table down at the far end, by one of the big windows. It was the perfect place to watch the rehearsal. If she glanced left, she was looking down on the football pitch. And if she looked straight ahead, through the glass wall in front of her, she was staring down into the main entrance hall. She wouldn't be able to hear what happened down there, but she would see everything.

She had only just settled in her seat when a car drew up outside the main entrance. Two welcomers stepped forward and opened the doors, standing to attention like sentries. The other welcomers formed an avenue leading into the school. At the top of the avenue was Tyler, with Robo beside him.

They both looked very small.

A moment later, they looked even smaller. The car door opened and out stepped the Headmaster. He glanced left and right, at the welcomers, and then strode into the school.

Tyler lifted his hand, pressing the button of the remote control, and Robo moved forward to face the

Headmaster. Lizzie couldn't hear him speaking, but she saw his hands lift, holding out a brightly coloured booklet that had to be the programme.

Surely the Prime Minister would smile? And say something nice to Tyler?

Obviously the Headmaster didn't think so. He gave a curt little nod and then followed Tyler and Robo as they led the way along the corridor towards the Maths rooms. Tyler looked completely calm and not at all nervous. For a second, Lizzie was surprised. Then she realized that was stupid. Of *course* he wasn't nervous. His mind was a total blank.

She couldn't see anything else for an hour or so, but she remembered some of the things Mrs Maron had said when she was reading out the programme. The Prime Minister would be going to the Maths room to see Emily Franklin, working on advanced Boolean algebra . . .

. . . then to the Biology lab, where Jakub Broz was dissecting a scorpion . . .

. . . then to the Art room, for a portrait to be painted by Carrie Adler—in twenty minutes . . .

Lizzie couldn't remember the next two or three things, but she knew Angelika was going to serve coffee at eleven o'clock (or was it ginger hot chocolate with honeycomb crumbs?). After that came the football match. At exactly eleven thirty.

The first part of the morning dragged. Lizzie was

supposed to be working on the paper she was writing, but she didn't even look at it. She knew her mind would go blank if she did, and she couldn't risk that. She needed to watch what happened on the football field.

At last it was half past eleven. Looking out of the window, she saw the welcomers bringing out chairs and arranging them in a row along the touchline. A moment later, the Headmaster came out, with Tyler and Robo behind him. He sat down in the middle chair—where the Prime Minister would be on Thursday. One of the welcomers offered him a blanket, but he waved it away impatiently.

No one offered Tyler anything. He just had to stand beside Robo.

The Headmaster lifted a hand, signalling that he was ready, and Mr Wasu came running out on to the field, with all the players behind him. They were tall and solid, more like young men than boys—except for Ethan. He was so small beside them that he looked ridiculous.

But not for long.

As soon as they started to play, Ethan was transformed. He seemed to be everywhere. Tackling boys twice his size. Dodging half a dozen others as he ran with the ball. Finding the perfect space to wait for a pass. And scoring. He scored two goals as Lizzie watched and set up two more.

It was beautiful to see. For a few moments, she actually felt sad at the thought of wrecking it all. There were dozens of people in the school who would have given anything to play like that.

But Ethan wasn't one of them. And it wasn't *real*.

That was why they had to stop the Prime Minister thinking Hazelbrook was perfect.

She still had hours to wait before her part of the rehearsal. Before the Prime Minister reached her, there was going to be a lunch in the staffroom (beautifully cooked by Roger Patterson and served by two boys and two girls in black clothes and white aprons). Then there would be three or four other people to meet before her turn came.

Mr Bains brought her a sandwich and a cup of tea at one o'clock. He hovered over her while she ate it and then whisked the mug away and swept up the crumbs— all three of them—with a brush and dustpan. Lizzie could see he was very, very nervous.

It was almost three o'clock when the Headmaster stalked into the information hub, with Tyler and Robo hurrying along behind him. He spent a few minutes looking round and then Mr Bains led him across to Lizzie's desk.

'As you see—' Mr Bains began.

'As you see, *Prime Minister*,' the Headmaster corrected, coldly.

'S-sorry,' Mr Bains stuttered. 'As you see, Prime Minister, Lizzie is making a detailed study of Shakespeare's grammar. Lizzie, please show the Prime

Minister your paper.'

Lizzie turned to the folder of papers beside—and her mind clouded over . . .

When she came to herself, the Headmaster was already walking out of the information hub. And everyone else was moving too, heading for the main hall, to hear Blake give the farewell speech. She picked up her bag and joined the procession.

As soon as they were all sitting down, the Headmaster stalked in, with Mrs Maron beside him. Tyler and Robo were behind, hurrying to keep up.

There was no sign of Blake. Not yet.

The Headmaster and Mrs Maron went up onto the stage. Tyler just managed to struggle up the steps with Robo and they went to stand behind the Headmaster's chair. Then Mrs Maron lifted her hand, signalling to someone in the wings.

And an extraordinary figure stepped out onto the stage.

It was Blake all right—there was no mistaking his face—but he was wearing a suit that completely disguised his shape. The green and purple jacket had huge shoulder pads, almost like wings. And the silver, sequinned trousers were so narrow they were more like leggings. They ended in long fringes that fell over the tops of his high-heeled purple boots. It was a stunning suit.

But not the kind of thing that Blake would ever wear.

He turned to face the Headmaster and began speaking in a loud, confident voice. What had Mrs Maron said? *Blake Vinney will deliver a farewell speech in Russian, Mandarin, and Arabic.* Lizzie couldn't understand a word he was saying. She didn't even know which language was which. But she could tell when he moved from one to another, because his accent changed dramatically.

It was an amazing, flamboyant performance. Lizzie was sure the Prime Minister was going to be very, very impressed—which made it even more important to have LOTS of disasters beforehand.

But there wasn't long to organize them. She was pleased with her idea for wrecking Ethan's football match, but she hadn't actually worked out how she was going to do it. She needed a bit of thinking time. On her own.

As Blake came to the end of his speech, she had her phone in her hand, ready to text Tyler. The Headmaster left the hall, escorted by the welcomers, and then everyone else began filing out, a row at a time. When the people in front of Lizzie stood up—hiding what she was doing—she started texting:

**Ok to go home without me Ty?**

He texted back just as she stood up.

**Fine**

Two minutes later, she was out of the building and heading for the High Street. She didn't really know what she was looking for, but perhaps she would spot something if she walked round the shops. A useful hint in a computer book. Or a DVD she could smuggle into school. There must be something she could use to make her idea work. There *must* be.

But there wasn't. Even if she'd had hundreds of pounds to spend, there was nothing useful, in any of the shops. She needed . . . she needed . . .

Think, think, *think* . . .

She was just about to give up and go home when she spotted Tyler. He was in the coffee shop next to the library—staring at the coffee machine behind the counter. Which was strange, because he didn't even *like* coffee.

She almost went in, to ask him what he was doing. But, just in time, she recognized the coffee machine. It was the same as the one Angelika had in the school canteen, and Tyler was staring at it as if he had to know exactly how it worked. Lizzie grinned to herself. It didn't take a genius to guess what he was up to. He must have ended up with the bit of paper that said *Angelika*. And he was planning to wreck her machine.

*Lucky Tyler*, she thought. He was bound to think up a really clever plan. But what about *her* plan? What was she going to do? Think, think, *think*.

She walked on down the High Street, frantically trying to work it out. Thinking so hard that she didn't notice anything around her—until she reached the narrow alley beside the bookshop.

As she drew level with it, a hand shot out from the entrance to the alley, clamping itself over her mouth. And a strong arm wrapped itself round her waist, pulling her off her feet and dragging her backwards into the darkness.

 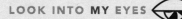

# 20

# SAFE TO TRUST?

Ethan was cycling the other way up the High Street. He saw Lizzie walking towards him and he stopped for a second, glancing round quickly, to see if it was safe to go up and speak to her.

When he looked back, she wasn't there. But where could she be? She hadn't had time to race ahead, into the bookshop, or dart backwards, into the clothes shop behind her. She'd just—vanished.

Ethan started cycling again, heading for the place where she'd disappeared. He'd only gone a couple of yards when he saw the dark space beyond the bookshop. He'd never noticed an alley there before, but that was what it had to be. And he didn't like the look of it. Why would Lizzie go down there?

He pedalled harder. And as he came level with the entrance, he saw Tyler coming out of a coffee shop further down the road. He waved at him, beckoning frantically. Then he turned into the alley, without waiting for Tyler to arrive.

Lizzie was down at the dark dead end of the alley, struggling with someone much taller and heavier than she was. He was hissing, 'Shh! *Shh!*' as he dragged her backwards. Ethan couldn't see his face, but he knew straight away who it was.

Blake.

Dropping his bike, Ethan raced down the alley and flung himself at Blake, hauling on the arm that was clamped round Lizzie's waist. But it was like trying to move a massive girder. He couldn't shift it an inch. And, all the time, Blake kept saying the same thing.

'Shh! *Shh!*'

At that moment, Tyler reached the top of the alley. 'No!' he yelled, when he saw them all. 'Don't hurt Lizzie!' He threw himself towards Blake, as if he was trying to rescue her all by himself.

But he didn't get a chance to do anything. Blake suddenly let go, and Lizzie and Ethan staggered backwards, crashing into the wall.

'I don't want to *hurt* anyone,' Blake said in an injured voice. As if he was amazed that Tyler could think that. 'I just want to *talk*.'

'Yes?' Lizzie shook her head and glared at him. 'Then why did you *attack* me?'

Blake shuffled his feet. 'OK, maybe I was a bit rough. But it had to be a secret. I didn't want anyone else to know I was talking to you.'

'Well, you've failed!' Lizzie snapped. 'Ethan and Tyler both know.'

'Oh, I don't mind *them*.' Blake said it as if she was stupid not to understand. 'They're part of your gang, aren't they? The people I want to talk to.'

'You do?' Ethan said cautiously. 'What do you want to talk about?'

Blake lowered his voice. 'School,' he muttered.

'OK, then.' Lizzie gave him a sharp look. 'Tell us what you think about it.'

Immediately, Blake's face rearranged itself into a simpering smile. 'Hazelbrook Academy is a brilliant school,' he said enthusiastically. 'It's helped me discover my true skills and my real ambition.' He clamped his mouth shut and the smile disappeared abruptly. He looked very, very miserable. And angry.

Ethan studied his face. Was this some kind of trap? Had the Headmaster sent Blake to spy on them? Lizzie was looking cautious too. But Tyler didn't give either of them time to think. His eyes opened wide and his mouth dropped open, as if he'd suddenly realized what was happening.

'It's that suit, isn't it?' he burst out. 'The one the textiles class made for you. You *hate* it.'

For a second, it looked as if Blake was going to say yes. Then the awful smile spread over his face again. 'It is a privilege to be modelling such elegant and well-made clothes,' he said.

Ethan thought quickly. 'OK. Don't try and tell us how *you* feel. Talk about me. How do you think I feel about playing football?'

'What's that got to do with anything?' Blake looked bewildered. 'You and football—that's a dream come true, isn't it? You're a natural genius. You must be over the moon.'

Lizzie sighed impatiently. 'No, that's how *you'd* feel if *you* were Ethan. But he's always been rubbish at football and he doesn't like sport anyway. So how do you think *he* feels?'

Blake's heavy face twisted into a frown, as if his brain was doing impossibly hard work. 'Must be . . . weird,' he said slowly. 'And . . . maybe he can't remember what he does? Maybe his mind's just empty. And if he tries to tell someone, there's this, this *pain—*' He stopped abruptly, as if he'd said more than he meant to.

'So what about you?' Ethan was watching him carefully. 'Can you remember talking Russian, and Mandarin, and Arabic?'

Blake started shaking his head. But only for a second. Then his face twisted in pain and he clapped his hands over his mouth. Ethan and Lizzie looked at each other.

'Do we trust him?' Ethan said.

Lizzie bit her lip. 'Maybe . . .'

They both looked back at Blake. 'So what's all this about?' Ethan said. 'What do you want us to do?'

'Got to get rid of *him*,' Blake muttered. 'That's when the school changed. When *he* came.'

'You mean the Headmaster?' said Lizzie.

Blake nodded. 'He's fixed it so we make him look good tomorrow. But suppose we make him look stupid instead—*really* stupid. He might go away then. And the school could get back to normal.'

'So you can start bullying Tyler again?' Lizzie said angrily.

'Oh. That.' Blake's face turned bright scarlet. 'I'm not . . . I mean, I won't . . . I mean . . .'

Lizzie went on staring at him without saying anything.

'Stop it, Liz,' Tyler said. 'Can't you see he's sorry? We ought to get him to help us.'

'Yes!' Lizzie said fiercely. 'Let's do that! Let's get someone to wreck his presentation—in a way that makes him look really, really stupid!'

She sounded so angry that Ethan took a step backwards. But Blake was nodding hard.

'Anything,' he said. 'I'll do anything.'

Lizzie suddenly went very still, as if she was working something out. 'Is that right?' she said. She looked round at Tyler and Ethan. 'You know, I think Blake *could* do something to help us. But I'll have to talk to him on my own.'

Ethan frowned. 'Are you sure?'

'Certain,' Lizzie said. And she stood and watched as he and Tyler walked away up the alley.

# 21

# THE LAST PIECE OF THE PLAN

When Ethan and Tyler were completely out of sight, Lizzie turned to Blake.

'Are you serious?' she said. 'You really want someone to wreck your presentation?'

He started nodding—and then stopped when the pain cut in. That was what convinced Lizzie. She was sure he wasn't faking.

'OK,' she said. 'I think I can arrange that. I'm not telling you who's going to do it—except it won't be me. And *you* have to do something first, to prove we can trust you.'

'Fair enough,' Blake said. 'What shall I do?'

Lizzie crossed her fingers. *Hope I was right about Tyler and the coffee machine.* 'You have to wreck what Angelika's doing tomorrow. She'll be serving coffee—or something—to the Prime Minister and you have to turn that into a disaster. But you mustn't tell her what you're doing. Right?'

Blake frowned for a moment. Lizzie could almost see his mind moving, working out why it had to be like that. At last he said, 'OK, I get it. And if I mess up the coffee break . . . ?'

'Then something really terrible will happen to spoil your Russian-Mandarin-Arabic speech. You won't get hurt. But I don't know what's going to happen, because it won't be me doing it. So you might end up looking even more stupid than you do in that suit.'

'I don't care,' Blake said doggedly. 'As long as the Headmaster looks like an idiot too.' He hesitated for a second and then stuck out his hand. 'So . . . are we friends now?'

It felt like the hardest thing she'd ever done, but Lizzie reached out and shook hands with him. His hand was so big it swamped hers. 'Friends,' she said.

Blake grinned. 'Then I'd better go and think about that coffee break, hadn't I?' And he loped off up the alley.

Lizzie waited until he'd gone. Then she walked out into the High Street and turned left, towards home. Tyler was waiting at the corner and he ran down to meet her.

'Are you OK?' he said nervously.

Lizzie nodded. 'I'm fine. But I need you to change what you're doing tomorrow. You're supposed to be wrecking Angelika's coffee break, aren't you?'

'You're not supposed to know that?' Tyler said accusingly. 'It's meant to be a secret.'

'I know,' Lizzie said. 'But I guessed. Anyway, you're not doing that any more. I've asked Blake to do it, to prove he's really on our side.'

'What about me?' Tyler looked disappointed. 'Don't I get to wreck anything?'

Lizzie grinned. 'You certainly do. If Blake messes up what Angelika's doing—and you'll be there to see if he does—I've promised him that someone will wreck his speech.'

'Meaning me?' Tyler looked terrified.

Lizzie nodded. 'He won't know it's you. And he says he doesn't care how silly he looks, as long as the Headmaster looks silly too.'

Tyler opened his mouth, as if he was going to argue. But he didn't. Suddenly, a huge smile spread across his face. 'Do you think he meant that? About not minding how silly he looks?'

Lizzie nodded and Tyler's smile got even bigger.

'Let's go home,' he said. 'There's something I need to do.'

'Me too,' said Lizzie. 'Do you think Dad will let me on the computer?'

She had to wait for that. When they got home, Dad was busy reading another message on the website. He looked up eagerly when they came in.

'This says: *Exceptional students will be making individual presentations to the Prime Minister*. Are you doing anything?'

'Both of us,' Tyler said. '*And* Robo. Mrs Maron made me leave him at school today, in case he got damaged. But he didn't mind. He's very keen to see the Prime Minister.'

*Careful*, Lizzie thought. *Don't overdo it*. But Dad was too excited to notice. He looked as if he was going to explode with pride. He nodded at Lizzie. 'Go in and tell Mum. She'll be thrilled.'

'I'll make her a cup of tea,' Lizzie said.

When she took in the tea, her mother was sitting up in bed, reading a book. She looked better than she'd looked for weeks. Lizzie carried the tea across to her bedside table and gave her a kiss.

'Dad said I should tell you, Tyler and I are both doing special things for the Prime Minister tomorrow.'

'That's wonderful,' her mother said. Then she looked carefully at Lizzie's face. 'You *are* pleased, aren't you?'

'It's a great honour,' Lizzie heard herself say. 'And a wonderful chance to show how Hazelbrook Academy produces students with special skills.'

'And what's the special skill you'll be showing off?' her mother said.

There was no point in thinking about what to say. The words came out automatically. 'I shall be presenting an analysis of Shakespeare's grammar, concentrating particularly on his use of the subjunctive.' *And please don't ask me about it, Mum. I don't want to tell you any more lies.*

Her mother looked startled, but she didn't ask any questions. She patted Lizzie's hand and said, 'You know we're proud of everything you do.'

Before she could say anything else, Dad called from the living room. 'Lizzie! Come and look at this!'

Mum smiled. 'He's very excited about the Prime Minister's visit. Go and see what he's found now.'

Lizzie turned to go. Then she looked back. 'Mum—do you think we should always do what's right? Even if it means getting into trouble?'

Her mother looked anxious. 'Is there something you want to tell me?'

'No.' Lizzie shook her head. 'I just wondered . . .'

Her mother hesitated. Then she said, 'It's important to think about it first. Very carefully. But in the end . . . yes. I always want you to do what you think is right.'

'Thank you,' Lizzie said.

*Now I just have to work out how.*

Mum patted her hand. 'Why don't you go and see what Dad's found on the computer?'

Lizzie gave her a grin and headed back to the living room. Dad was beckoning and pointing at the screen.

'It's your football team!' he said. 'Who's the tiny little guy?'

Lizzie went round to look over his shoulder. There was the school first team, lined up in the changing room. Dad was right. Ethan did look ridiculously small next to the others.

But that wasn't why she leaned forward suddenly, staring hard at the photograph. It wasn't because of Ethan that her heart gave a thump and a voice in her mind shrieked, *Yes!* She'd spotted something else, behind the footballers. Something that solved all her problems.

Hanging down from the changing room ceiling was a projector, set up ready to show one of Mr Wasu's 'training' videos. And below it, on a table, was a school laptop—with a little blue memory stick plugged in on one side.

There was nothing special about it. It was one of the standard school memory sticks. Exactly like the ones Dad had been given, which were still lying in a little pile on the coffee table.

Lizzie straightened up. 'Why don't *we* have some tea too?' she said. She laid out three coasters on the table, brushing the memory sticks to one side—and slipping one of them into her hand. 'I'll go and get it.'

In the kitchen, she dropped the memory stick into her pocket and reached for three mugs. All she needed now was a chance to use the computer, without being watched.

She had to wait until six o'clock. Dad always watched the news then, which gave her half an hour to find the sort of video she wanted and copy it on to the memory stick.

She just managed it in time. As she took the memory stick out of the computer, Dad turned round from the television.

'You've been busy,' he said. 'What are you doing?'

'Something for tomorrow,' Lizzie said truthfully. 'But I've finished now. Want me to help with the cooking?'

'You could peel some potatoes,' Dad said.

*Perfect*, Lizzie thought. She needed some peace and quiet, to think about her next problem.

How was she going to get the memory stick into Mr Wasu's computer?

## 22

# SABOTAGE

Then it was Thursday morning.

Ethan left home half an hour early. He had to get to school before Tyler, because he needed some time alone with Robo. Not long. Just a few minutes.

There were a couple of policemen at the school gate, with a dog. Ethan gave them a grin as he got off his bike.

'You're bright and early,' one of them said. 'Let's have a quick look in your bag.'

That was easy. There was nothing in there except his football kit. The policeman gave him an approving grin as he rummaged through it.

'You must be good,' he said, 'if they're letting you play today.'

'No,' Ethan said lightly. 'I'm rubbish.'

Both policemen laughed and the one with the dog patted Ethan's shoulder. 'Yeah, I bet,' he said. 'We'll be over later on, to see you make a fool of yourself.'

Once he was through the gate, everything was easy. It was easy to dodge the drones, because most of them were outside, monitoring people arriving. He kept a good lookout for the rest as he headed for the computer engineering room.

Robo was standing in the far corner, with his head bent down because he was switched off. Ethan glanced round—doing a final drone check—and then hurried across to him.

He was very quick, because he'd worked it all out in advance. He started a text to David and Jatinder, his two computer geek friends from his last school.

**Something for U 2 watch and share starts 11am**

He added the link, then sent the text. Then he turned on the camera and started streaming the video.

'Here you are,' he whispered to Robo, as he pushed the phone into the docking slot on the robot's chest. 'Take care of it.'

He was pretty sure no one would spot it. It was the same silver colour as Robo's casing and its small, dark lens just added one more black dot to the complicated bank of controls and dials on the robot's front panel. The only person who might have noticed the difference was Tyler. And he wasn't going to notice anything, because his mind would be a total blank while he was with the Prime Minister.

Ethan stepped back and took a last look at Robo. 'You'd better get this right, robot,' he muttered. 'I'm counting on you.'

Then he slipped out of the room and headed down to registration.

Lizzie and Tyler were early too. They turned up five minutes after Ethan and they were almost at the gate when Lizzie spotted the two policemen there.

'They're checking people's bags,' she whispered to

Tyler. 'Is there anything in yours you don't want them to find?'

'It's in my pocket,' he whispered back. 'Do you think they'll check there?'

Lizzie shook her head, wondering what it was. But she knew she mustn't ask.

The policemen glanced quickly into their bags then looked up and grinned. 'Enjoy your day!' one of them said. 'Got anything special to show the Prime Minister?'

'My robot,' Tyler said. 'I designed him myself.'

The other policeman shook his head in wonder. 'This school! What is it like?'

*You wouldn't believe it if I told you,* Lizzie thought. She smiled back at the policemen and gave Tyler a nudge. They had to get inside the school building as quickly as they could.

'Be careful,' she muttered as they went through the door.

Tyler nodded, gave her a cheeky, excited grin and disappeared up the corridor towards the hall.

Lizzie watched him for a second, hoping he wasn't going to do anything stupid. Then she turned the other way, keeping a careful lookout for drones. The only one she saw was going the other way. She let it pass her, waited until it was round the corner, and then ran down the corridor to the changing rooms.

There was no time to hesitate, no time to wonder what she would do if anyone saw her going into the boys' changing room. She just raced in, spotted the computer, and ran across to it, feeling so nervous she could hardly breathe.

What if there was no memory stick there?

What if Mr Wasu had taken it home, to keep it safe?

What if someone came in while she was swapping it?

What if . . .?

But everything was all right. There was a little blue memory stick in one of the USB ports. Exactly like the memory stick in her hand. It only took her a second to swap them over and push the one she'd taken into her pocket.

As she turned to go, she heard someone outside, in the corridor. Sprinting across the changing room, she unlocked the outside door, ran through it, and dodged along the wall of the building, getting out of sight as fast as she could. There was no way of locking the door again. She just had to hope no one would notice.

It took her ten minutes to stroll along the edge of the football field and right round the building, to join the crowd of people at the front door.

That was lucky. It meant she wasn't in the information hub when Angelika ran in, looking frazzled and anxious.

Mr Bains gave her a friendly smile and shook his head. 'Nice to see you, Angelika, but I don't think you should be here. Aren't you supposed to be in the canteen, getting ready for the coffee break?'

'That's just *it*,' Angelika wailed. 'There's something I need to look up—in case the Prime Minister asks me about the coffee. I forgot to do it yesterday.'

'No problem,' said Mr Bains. 'What do you need?'

'It's OK,' Angelika said quickly. 'I know where it is.'

She ran across the room to the table in the far corner and pulled down the book she'd spotted yesterday. *Farming in Colombia*. She put it down on the table— right next to a thick folder labelled *Please leave this here. Thanks. Lizzie.*

For a couple of seconds, while Mr Bains was watching her, she bent over the book, staring at a page of information about Colombian coffee exports. But as soon as he looked away, she pulled a paper bag out of her coat pocket.

Carefully, she began to slip things between the sheets of paper in Lizzie's folder . . .

At exactly the same moment, a football went shooting across the canteen and hit the counter in front of Angelika's coffee machine.

Mrs Foster opened the sliding doors between the kitchen and the serving counter. 'WHAT WAS THAT???' she yelled.

'I'm sorry. I'm really, really sorry.' Blake sidled into the canteen, looking polite and apologetic. 'The ball just slipped out of my hands.'

'No footballs in here,' Mrs Foster said grumpily. 'Health and safety.'

'Yes. Of course. I'll get it straight away.' Blake hurried across the canteen.

As he bent down to pick up the ball, he heard the sliding doors crash together again. Good. Mrs Foster had gone back to cooking the lunch. Quickly, he reached over the coffee counter, picking up two jars of brown powder from Angelika's worktop.

As he took off the lids, he smiled . . .

Tyler was smiling too. He was standing in the hall, beaming all over his face—right underneath a drone.

'Tyler Warren—you're an idiot!' he said. 'Why were you struggling up the front steps to get Robo onto the stage? Duh!'

He ran forward and disappeared through the door at the side of the stage. For a few seconds, he was out of sight of the drone. Then he appeared from the wings, walking onto the stage with an even bigger grin.

'That's much better!' he said. 'Now I won't look stupid in front of the Prime Minister!'

He clapped his hands as he jumped off the stage and ran out of the hall.

Now everything was ready for the Prime Minister's visit. . .

## 23

# PMV

It was ten o'clock when the Prime Minister's car drew up outside the school, with a line of other cars behind it. Looking down from her seat in the information hub, Lizzie felt for a second as if she'd gone back to yesterday. There was the same double line of welcomers, forming an avenue into the school. Tyler and Robo were standing at the end of the avenue, in exactly the same place as before. And the same two welcomers stepped forward, opening the car door and then standing to attention, like sentries.

Then the Prime Minister stepped out of the car—and suddenly everything was different from yesterday. Not because there were extra people jumping out of the other cars, with cameras and notebooks and briefcases, but because the Headmaster was there. Not pretending to be someone else, but *shaking the Prime Minister's hand*.

For the first time, Lizzie understood the real danger. The Prime Minister was going to be in the school for hours. With the Headmaster. At any moment, the Headmaster could take off his dark glasses . . . and what would happen then?

*We'd better have got it right*, she thought, as the Prime Minister walked into the school. Tyler and Robo came forward and she held her breath, waiting for the first disaster. She didn't know who was supposed to be wrecking Tyler's star turn, but it had to be *spectacular*.

Nothing happened.

Everything was exactly the same as yesterday. Tyler pressed the button of the remote control, Robo moved forward, holding out the programme booklet, and the Prime Minister took it, looking pleased and impressed.

Lizzie's heart sank like a lump of lead in her chest. She hardly noticed the Prime Minister smiling and saying nice things to Tyler. All she could think was, *It's gone wrong. The first bit of the plan hasn't worked.*

As the Headmaster led the way out of the entrance hall, she dropped her head into her hands, imagining the Prime Minister walking round the school. Being impressed by Emily Franklin and her Boolean algebra. Admiring the way Jakub Broz did his dissection. Gasping with amazement at the portrait Carrie Adler was going to paint.

By the time they reached the canteen, for their coffee break, the Prime Minister would be saying the same as everyone else—even without being hypnotized: *Hazelbrook Academy is a brilliant school!*

At eleven o'clock, Angelika's heart started sinking, like Lizzie's. When the Headmaster ushered the Prime Minister into the canteen, she saw Robo behind them— working perfectly. The Headmaster looked cold and controlled, as he always did, but the Prime Minister was smiling and saying, 'Astounding!' and 'Never seen anything like it!'

That shouldn't be happening. Things should have started going wrong, from the very beginning. Someone should have wrecked Robo . . .

Before she could finish the thought, her mind went blank. 'Coffee, Prime Minister?' she said brightly.

The Prime Minister hesitated, looking up at the notice above the counter. 'Maybe I could try the special ginger hot chocolate instead? Is it your own invention?'

Angelika's teeth flashed white as she smiled. 'It's our signature drink. It will be my pleasure to make it for you.'

Mrs Maron appeared, coming up behind the Prime Minister. 'Please, take a seat.' She gestured at one of the comfortable padded chairs that had been specially brought in and she, the Prime Minister, and the Headmaster all sat down together round a spotless glass coffee table. Tyler and Robo moved into position behind them as Angelika warmed the milk and mixed in the chocolate powder.

When she had piped a big swirl of whipped cream on top of the mug, she reached for the honeycomb crumbs. Unscrewing the jar, she took a big spoonful of the brown powder and sprinkled it over the cream, spelling out WELCOME, in big letters. That took a lot of crumbs. By the time she'd finished, the jar was almost empty.

Picking up the mug, she walked out from behind the counter. 'Enjoy!' she cooed, as she handed over the hot chocolate.

The Prime Minister smiled at her, lifted the mug,

took a long swig of the honeycomb, whipped cream, and hot chocolate and—

'YEEEEUGGGHHH!!!!'

A long jet of hot chocolate shot out across the table, hitting Mrs Maron on the chest, in the middle of her smart blue jacket. There was a pool of hot chocolate on the glass tabletop too. The Prime Minister put the mug down in the middle of it, gasping like a goldfish.

The Headmaster turned on Angelika. *'What have you done?'* he said, in a terrible voice.

Angelika's mind cleared suddenly and she blinked round at them all. What on earth had happened? Why was the Prime Minister gasping and moaning? Why was her mum's jacket covered in hot chocolate and cream?

Mrs Maron reached across to the Prime Minister's mug and scooped up a fingerful of whipped cream and honeycomb crumbs. Carefully, she stuck out her tongue and tasted it. Then she wiped her mouth, hard, with the back of her other hand.

'Curry powder!' she said. 'It's not honeycomb at all. It's *very strong curry powder.'*

'Get some water! Quickly!' the Headmaster snapped.

Angelika ran across to the counter and filled a big glass with cold water, trying not to smile. She was going to be in terrible trouble—but it was worth it.

She didn't know who had wrecked her star turn, but they'd done a brilliant job.

Lizzie didn't know what had happened in the canteen,

but she could tell something had gone wrong. Looking down at the football field, she saw the welcomers laying out the chairs on the touchline at exactly twenty five past eleven. Right on time. But it was another fifteen minutes before the Headmaster appeared with the Prime Minister.

They were running late.

As the Headmaster showed the Prime Minister to a seat, Mr Bains slipped across the room and sat down in the chair next to Lizzie's. 'We've got a grandstand view,' he said, giving her a grin.

Lizzie smiled back, but under the table, her hands were clenched into tight little fists. This was her moment. Her chance to wreck part of the day.

Would her plan work?

The Headmaster lifted a hand, signalling that it was time to start. Instantly, Mr Wasu came through the door from the changing room.

But he didn't run, the way he had in the rehearsal. He walked on, very elegantly, with his legs straight and his toes pointed. Flapping his arms like wings. And behind him came a long line of boys—both football teams and the two reserves as well.

They were running, but not like footballers. Their legs were straight too, and their toes were as pointed as toes *could* be, in football boots. And at every fifth step, they hopped on one toe, spreading their arms wide as they zigzagged across the pitch.

'What are they doing?' Mr Bains said in a baffled voice. 'Is it some kind of warm-up?'

Lizzie didn't dare to speak, in case she laughed out loud. The footballers all had earnest expressions, as if they were trying hard to look graceful. But every time they went up on their points, three or four of them fell over. Which wasn't surprising.

It's not really possible to dance *Swan Lake* in football boots.

The Headmaster was on his feet now, shouting at them all, but it looked as if they couldn't stop. They made a ragged square and then galumphed into a circle, bumping into each other as they tripped and fell. Next they formed a triangle, with Ethan in the centre front, at the apex.

He went up on one pointed toe, staggered—and fell over backwards.

As he fell, he crashed into the people behind him and they fell over too, knocking into the people behind *them*. Then the next row went over, and the next, until all twenty-four boys were lying flat on their backs in the mud.

Lizzie couldn't see the Headmaster's face, but she could tell he was furious. He stood up, signalling to the Prime Minister that they were leaving. Immediately. They walked off the field, with Tyler and Robo hurrying along behind them.

Lizzie wasn't sure, but she thought the Prime Minister was laughing.

Mr Bains was almost speechless with amazement. 'What—what was going on there?' he stuttered. 'What were they *doing*?'

Lizzie shrugged and tried to look amazed too. She certainly wasn't going to answer his questions, but they kept her busy for the rest of the morning. He went on and on about what had happened to the footballers, and all she had to do was keep saying, 'Yes, it was weird' and 'Maybe it was *meant* to be funny.'

The questions kept Mr Bains busy too, which was good. Otherwise, he might have told her to open her folder and check her presentation and she had no intention of doing that before the Prime Minister came. She didn't want to miss anything.

It was just before two o'clock when the Headmaster ushered the Prime Minister into the information hub.

'They're early!' Mr Bains said, panicking. 'They're not supposed to be here for another hour.'

'It's because of the football,' Lizzie said. 'They didn't stay till the end.' (*Which was a real pity*, she thought. The boys had gone on dancing for ages, with no one watching except her.)

Mr Bains went rushing over to the door, to greet the Prime Minister, and Lizzie looked at her folder.

She had no idea what was inside, except that it was something about Shakespeare and grammar. Someone— either Ethan or Angelika—was supposed to be turning that into a disaster, but she couldn't think how. She didn't know what she was going to do, but surely it was all talking? How could anyone interfere with that?

Now Mr Bains was ushering the Prime Minister towards her, with the Headmaster stalking along behind. And Tyler and Robo trailing after them.

'As you will see, Prime Minister,' Mr Bains was saying, 'Lizzie has made an impressive, in-depth study of Shakespeare's language.'

Lizzie reached for the folder. Had someone scribbled in a lot of jokes? Or something rude? That wasn't going to be much of a disaster. The Prime Minister was hardly going to read the whole folder, so it didn't really matter what it said. She was only going to . . .

Then her mind clouded over. So she missed what came next . . .

She didn't know she was smiling up at the Prime Minister. Didn't hear herself say, 'I have been studying Shakespeare's grammar, particularly his use of the subjunctive.' Her eyes were shining, as if that was the most fascinating thing in the world. 'Would you like to take a look at my graphs, and the paper I've written?'

The Prime Minister nodded politely, and she picked up the folder in one hand and swung round with it.

If she hadn't been on autopilot, she might have noticed that the folder was surprisingly heavy. But she didn't. She just held it out eagerly—and all the things Angelika had slipped inside came flying out. The Prime Minister was hit by

a slice of bread and honey,

a small pizza margherita,

a half-melted chocolate biscuit,

a red jam tart, and

a cold fried egg.

For a second, even the Headmaster was speechless.

He stood and watched as the egg slid slowly down the Prime Minister's jacket and hit the floor with a soft, greasy *plop*.

When Lizzie came round, Mr Bains was on his knees, scraping jam off the carpet. There was no one else in the room.

'What—what happened?' she said.

Mr Bains didn't answer. He just shook his head, as if he was beyond words.

Lizzie looked at her watch. She wanted to help him, but she had to be in the hall, to see if Tyler managed to wreck Blake's speech. She picked up her bag and looked down at Mr Bains.

'Let's clear up later,' she said. 'We mustn't miss Blake.'

While Mr Bains was still getting up off his knees, she ran out of the information hub and joined the long line of people filing along the corridor. When she reached the hall, it was almost full. She found an empty chair, right at the back, but she hardly had time to sit down before everyone stood up.

The Headmaster led the Prime Minister into the hall, followed first by Mrs Maron and then by Tyler and Robo. As they went past Lizzie, she stared at the Prime Minister's jacket.

*It's a different one*, she thought. *That's strange.* But she had no idea why. Tyler didn't even glance towards her. *He probably doesn't even know it's me,* she thought sadly.

But—wait a minute. If Tyler's mind was blank, how could he ruin Blake's speech? He wouldn't even know it was happening.

The Headmaster ushered the Prime Minister onto the platform, waited a few seconds, to let Robo and Tyler get into their place behind, and then gave the signal for the speech to begin.

When Blake stepped out of the wings, the Prime Minister looked startled for a second. Lizzie wasn't surprised. The special clothes looked even more spectacular than she'd remembered. The shoulder pads seemed bigger and the trousers glittered more brightly. They weren't spoilt at all. For a second, she felt sick with disappointment.

Moving into position, Blake started the Russian part of his speech. The Prime Minister looked down at the programme booklet and gave a small, approving nod. Everything was going horribly right.

And then Blake started wriggling.

It began at his shoulders. He raised first one and then the other, making the huge shoulder pads bob up and down. Then he bent down and rubbed his knees, pulling at the sequinned trouser legs.

His voice was still clear and steady, carrying on with the speech, but nothing else about him was still. He scratched at his elbows, through the velvet sleeves of his jacket, then lifted the bottom of the jacket, pulling it away from his waist.

The Headmaster stood up, as if he was going to

interrupt. But before he could say a word, Blake switched from Russian to Mandarin—and ripped off the green and purple jacket. He threw the jacket on the ground and then tore at the green silk shirt he was wearing underneath, bursting all the buttons.

'Stop that!' the Headmaster shouted.

But it was no use. Declaiming in fluent Mandarin, Blake wrenched at his high-heeled purple boots, pulling them off and throwing them into the wings. Then he peeled off the tight, glittering trousers, tugging his feet free.

Now he wasn't wearing anything except a pair of bright red boxer shorts.

'Stop!' the Headmaster thundered frantically. And then, '*Wake up!*'

Blake froze for a second—then blinked and looked down at himself. His mouth dropped open.

The Headmaster stood up, heading towards him, but there was no need. With a loud squeal, Blake charged off the stage and disappeared into the wings.

Almost everyone in the hall was laughing now. But not Lizzie. She was watching Tyler. When the Headmaster had said, 'Wake up!', he'd blinked—just like Blake—and then glanced left and right, looking dazed. As his eyes reached Robo, he'd stopped suddenly, staring at Robo's chest with a puzzled expression.

What had he seen?

As Blake disappeared off the stage, Tyler leaned forward and took hold of something, pulling it out of Robo's front panel. The moment she saw it, Lizzie knew what it was.

*Ethan's phone!*

The Headmaster saw the movement too, out of the corner of his eye. When he realized what Tyler was holding, he turned round and swept towards him, with both hands outstretched. But before he could grab the phone, Ethan stood up, halfway down the hall.

'Here, Tyler!' he yelled. 'Throw it to me!'

Tyler flung the phone at him, as hard as he could. Ethan raced forward and caught it, just before it hit the ground. Then he turned and ran towards the back of the hall.

'Welcomers!' shouted the Headmaster. 'Catch that boy!'

The welcomers were sitting all down the sides of

the hall. They stood up and raced to the back, only just behind Ethan.

Lizzie stood up and shouted. 'Go, Ethan! You're faster than they are! I've seen you on the football pitch!' She struggled along the row and ran after the welcomers. If they cornered Ethan, she had to be there.

She'd only been running for a few seconds when Blake overtook her, pulling on his school shirt.

'Let's do it!' he panted. 'Let's rescue him!'

Lizzie glanced over her shoulder and saw Angelika coming too. And then Tyler—oh goodness!—*sitting on Robo's shoulders*! He was waving the remote control and pressing the same button, again and again.

'Faster, Robo! Faster!' he was shouting.

She could see the welcomers in front, streaming across the main entrance hall. And Ethan, only a few steps ahead now, running out of the front door and down the steps.

What was he doing? Where was he going?

He raced across the tarmac to the school's main gates and started to climb them. By the time the welcomers reached him, he was sitting on top of the gates, looking at his phone.

One of the welcomers started to climb after him, but Blake was there. He grabbed the boy's legs and pulled him down again.

'Leave Ethan alone!' he bellowed. 'He's on our side!'

'Yes, leave him alone!' shouted Tyler. He and Robo zoomed right into the middle of the crowd, knocking welcomers right and left.

'Someone's going to get hurt!' wailed Angelika. 'We've got to stop them.'

She and Lizzie struggled forward, dodging the welcomers who were all staggering backwards, one by one, as Blake threw them out of the way. When Lizzie reached Tyler, he was just sliding down from Robo's shoulders. She pulled them both backwards, until they were right against the gates.

In a couple of seconds, Angelika and Blake were beside them. They all stood in a row, facing the welcomers, with Ethan above their heads, on top of the gate.

And then Ethan said, 'The Headmaster!'

He was coming down the steps from the main entrance. As he walked towards them, he looked perfectly calm. He stopped when he reached the welcomers and looked up scornfully at Ethan.

'You're wasting your time,' he said. His eyes travelled down to stare at Lizzie. Angelika. Blake. Tyler. And Robo. 'You're all wasting your time.'

'No, we're not!' Tyler said. 'We spoilt your stupid programme. Angelika's hot chocolate went wrong, and so did Ethan's football match. Lizzie covered the Prime Minister with food and everyone laughed at Blake.'

'The Prime Minister won't give you any more schools to run!' Angelika said. 'Not after today.'

'No?' said the Headmaster.

There was something in his voice that made Lizzie shiver. He didn't sound defeated. He sounded as though he'd got everything he wanted. What had he done?

He waited until everyone was completely still. Then he said, 'I have just been talking to the Prime Minister. And to the advisors and journalists and photographers who came to report on today's visit. For ten minutes, I had their full attention.'

Then Lizzie knew what he'd done. 'You've hypnotized them all, haven't you? It doesn't matter what *really* happened today. You've made them all believe it was wonderful.'

The Headmaster smiled. An ugly, triumphant smile. 'They have all agreed that today was a triumph, for the school and for my method of education. The Prime Minister will be making an announcement next Wednesday. My plans will go ahead, exactly as I intended.'

*It's over*, Lizzie thought. *It's all over*.

The Headmaster looked up at Ethan, stretching out a long, pale hand towards him. 'I'm sure you felt very clever, using the robot to carry your phone round and film what happened. But no one will ever see that video. Give me the phone.'

At last Lizzie understood Ethan's plan. It would have been brilliant—if he'd pulled it off. But it had failed—like all their other plans. She felt like bursting into tears.

Ethan held his phone high in the air for a moment. Then he dropped it into the Headmaster's outstretched hand. The Headmaster dropped the phone onto the path, grinding it into the tarmac with the heel of his left shoe. Lizzie heard the screen splinter.

She looked back at Ethan, expecting him to be devastated. But he wasn't.

He was smiling.

'You're too late!' he said, grinning down at the Headmaster. 'The pictures are out there already!'

'What?' The Headmaster looked up, startled.

Ethan gave a shout of laughter. 'I've been live-streaming the video all day! And it's gone viral. It's trending all over the internet. There's no way you can stop that now.'

The Headmaster's face turned purple with fury. He was too angry to speak.

'We've won!' Tyler yelled at the Headmaster. 'We've beaten you!'

The Headmaster glared round at them all. 'You are foolish, despicable children!' he said scornfully. 'You have rejected the chance to be part of my plans—and you will regret it! Order will triumph! *I will not be defeated!*'

Before anyone could answer, there was a loud *click* from the gates and they started swinging open, carrying Ethan with them. Lizzie looked round at the school car park and saw a line of shiny black cars heading towards them.

'The Prime Minister's leaving!' she said.

Everyone else turned to look. As the first car reached the gates, the rear window slid down and the Prime Minister looked out, waving goodbye.

'Goodbye!' Lizzie shouted back. 'Don't forget to check all the social media!'

As the car slid through the gates, the Prime Minister was frowning anxiously and pulling out a phone.

Angelika clapped her hands. 'Ethan, you're a genius!'

Lizzie nodded. 'There's no way the Prime Minister's going to make that announcement on Wednesday. Not now.'

'Unless it's about a new Head for Hazelbrook,' Blake said, grinning all over his face.

Tyler laughed. 'What do you think about *that*?' he said, turning back to look at the Headmaster.

But the Headmaster was nowhere to be seen.

'He must have gone while we were watching the Prime Minister's car,' said Blake.

'Good!' Angelika said fiercely. 'Let's hope we never see him again!'

Tyler and Blake started laughing and cheering, but Lizzie looked up at Ethan. Their eyes met, and she knew they were thinking the same thing. *If only we could be sure . . .*

'So how did it go?' said her mother, as Lizzie walked into the bedroom. 'I kept hearing Dad yell at the computer, but none of it made any sense—except the bit about your Headmaster getting the sack.'

Lizzie gave her a massive grin. 'I'll tell you all about it in a bit. But I need to go and make some tea first. We've brought some friends home with us. Is that OK?'

'It's wonderful,' her mother said. 'Can I come out and say hello?'

'Oh, yes!' Lizzie said.

Mum swung her legs out of bed and pulled on a dressing-gown. Then she walked slowly across the hall and into the living room.

'Mum!' Tyler jumped up and hugged her. 'These are our best friends, Ethan and Angelika and Blake. They've been doing fantastic things today.'

Lizzie stuck her head round the door. 'And Robo. Don't forget him. He was really important.'

Dad was staring at the computer, shaking his head. 'It was chaos. Absolute chaos.' He looked round at Blake. 'Especially your speech at the end. What were you *doing*?'

'No idea,' Blake grinned. 'And I don't know who made it happen. But it was *sensational*!'

'It was me,' Tyler said proudly. 'I did it by magic.'

'By *magic*?' Ethan raised his eyebrows. 'That's impossible.'

'No it's not.' Tyler started laughing. 'I filled Blake's special suit with itching powder from my magic set. And it worked like—like a charm!'

Mum sat down at the table, next to Dad. 'I think you'd better tell us all about it,' she said. 'From the very beginning.'

# Ready for more great stories?

## CAN YOU RESIST . . . ?